A TIME OF WITCHES

A TIME OF WITCHES

Book Two
A Mindful Things Series

Mya Duong

Arborville House

ISBN: 978-0-9993346-2-1 (paperback)
ISBN: 978-0-9993346-3-8 (ebook)

FIRST EDITION

For Danica—

We never know our time until it's gone.
Always in our hearts.

Contents

PROLOGUE

As I walked through the garden, a sweetness wrapped me in her warm and loving embrace. The sky smiled down upon me as the air trickled words into my ear with sounds I longed to know. But she couldn't speak freely; her idyllic voice silenced. I didn't care; I belonged here. I floated, and I remained free. I roamed as the lady of the garden.

Everything brimmed with life. Everything felt perfect and right. I moved closer to the home that summoned me. I reached out to her.

"Here I am." The sound of my voice floated on the air.

A shadow confronted me, then disappeared. The sky frowned down at me. The wind snapped against my skin. I ran.

"Wait for me," I cried.

She hissed and roiled, her words indistinguishable.

"Tell me!" I called out as I fell to the ground. My breath lapsed, and I grew tired. The garden transformed, no longer mine.

I reached for the light. His strength pulled me up. His gaze reflected warmth and kindness; his brightness showered me with hope. The stranger guided me home, but my home moved further and further away. She wore a different face. The stranger pulled me ahead, ignoring the anger brewing in the sky. We stopped.

Someone lurked in the shadows. He wore a mask. His anger erupted. He yanked at my arm. I pulled away, but he wouldn't release me.

The wind stormed through my once beautiful garden. She shouted her warnings. She screamed her fears. I faced the darkness again, but found only sorrow. And pain. Reaching for the light, I looked at him with pleading eyes. All I found was emptiness. My eyes fixed on the horror in front of me.

The house was burning! My home was on fire! The flames shot out everywhere. I stood frozen as I watched. She collapsed to the ground.

"Nooo!"

"Lauren! Lauren, wake up!"

1

TIME ZONE

"C'mon, Lauren. You're going to miss your flight. It'll be here when you get back," Raegan urged me. She watched me pack and unpack the same items. Even Oscar barked at me.

"I know. I'm almost ready. Just a few more things to check over, and I'm off." I ran through the list in my head of the immediate necessities, making sure not to over pack. Extreme. I planned to avoid it at all cost.

"Quinn is waiting for you downstairs. He seems preoccupied. The bag he's carrying looks like a survivor's kit," she remarked.

"He's just nervous about flying." I placed the special box in my backpack and secured the bracelet to my wrist. "He likes to travel light. I'm sure his suitcase is in the car."

"I still don't know why you're taking some of these things, instead of leaving them behind." She pointed to a first aid kit and a pair of running shoes. "It's not like you'll be gone that long."

"I just want to take it with me." I grabbed the final items—a raincoat and thermal underwear—things I wouldn't wear in the hot month of August.

"Lauren, why are you leaving behind your newer dresses

and your swimsuit?" Raegan dangled clothes in my face.

"I won't need them. We'll be doing low keys things like hiking. Wear them if you want."

She shrugged. "You don't have to tell me twice."

I'd almost forgotten something important in the midst of all our planning and rushing around. I gave Raegan a long and suffocating hug. I missed her already.

"Cut it out, Lauren. I can't breathe," she gasped, pushing me away. "Why the long goodbyes? I'll see you in a week."

"Sure. See you then."

I sprinted downstairs to find Quinn pacing, the keys in his hand. He appeared apprehensive, carrying his backpack filled with who-knows-what.

"We should get out of here. I'll have to move quickly in order to make good time." He rushed out the door before I could say anything. I climbed into the black Volkswagen, not even buckled up before he took off.

I glanced back, the house getting smaller and my friends' place even more distant. Emptiness consumed me. The feeling lingered, stalling until it crept into my heart. *My home.*

"We're going to be okay," Quinn said, squeezing my hand.

I nodded. "I know." I clung to my bag.

"Highway fourteen should be clear," he mumbled, eyes steady on the road. The speedometer went from thirty-to-fifty. We hadn't even reached the highway yet.

I triple checked my bag to ensure I'd packed all the necessary items. I touched the contents of my wallet. "Do you think we have enough money?"

"We'll be fine. I made several withdrawals before the trip, and we can stop at an ATM if we need more money. It should last us a while as long as we're careful." Quinn glanced at me, but I refused to show any doubt. He turned back to the endless road. "We have everything we need."

"I guess you're right. I'm surprised they still want to go to Connecticut," I said. My thoughts traveled to my original home.

"It's important to your parents."

I knew they wanted to go even if my memory never returned. "They have people watching Mercedes and Nicholas. They've kept a low profile since the party incident."

"Better to not draw attention until they make their next move. Leaving you alone after their plans fell apart is what I think they're doing," Quinn said. "I wish I knew their next plan."

"I'll take *leaving me alone* any day. I just hope my parents will let us go."

Quinn didn't say anything else. His eyes remained on the road. Silence fell over us for the rest of the trip.

O'Hare lurked in the distance. Quinn drove faster toward the maze-like airport. I held onto my seat as he weaved in and out of the traffic headed to the parking lot.

"They should be inside. Let's get our stuff," he said.

I jumped out of the car and grabbed my carryon and the medium-sized rolling suitcase. We managed the ticketing process without delay.

The gate number for New Haven stood out—C34. My parents, Chelsea, and Isaak looked up as we inched closer to the gate. Mom waved to us.

"Just in time with moments to spare," I said.

"We knew you'd be on time," Dad responded. He attempted to read my face, but I turned away.

"I'll take the window seat in the exit row since you don't seem to care," Isaak said to Chelsea. "I don't know why

Mom chose not to purchase extra leg room. Good thing this is a short flight. The layover in Philly should be enough time to stretch out and leave."

Chelsea pierced through Isaak's happy-go-lucky nature. "It's to avoid making you the center of attention."

He ignored her. "Having more leg room isn't going to kill. In fact, I'd take a direct flight any day. The sooner we get to New Haven, the better."

Quinn nodded. "I agree. The only time that I've ever been to Philadelphia was hectic. The right family wasn't there." Quinn glanced at me.

"It's not so bad. It has its perks. But it can be tough like Chicago," Isaak replied.

"He meant something else," Chelsea remarked.

"I know that. I was just commenting on how the two cities are alike. Is that *okay* with you?"

Chelsea sneered at him.

Isaak gave Chelsea a reproachful look. "It would've been ideal if they'd purchased first class seats. That would keep us away from everyone."

"Why would they do that, genius? Again, that would draw attention. Like you said, it's not a long flight and having a stop shouldn't put you over the edge," she remarked in a low voice. "You'll survive. Besides, I didn't see you fork over the money for the luxury seats."

"It wasn't *my* idea to go. I would've picked California or Hawaii for a family trip. At least we could have some *real* fun and not a working trip," Isaak retorted, his face inches from Chelsea's. "Don't you think it's rather morbid to continually go to Connecticut? Why don't we just let the past stay in the past?"

"Because the past keeps creeping up on us, and until we

take care of the issues, it's always going to be a part of us whether you like it or not," Chelsea replied.

"I realize that, but for once can't we let it slide and have a normal family vacation without being on guard? If they find us, they'll find us."

Chelsea fumed. I'd never seen her get worked up over a flight and a trip to Connecticut. Like Dad, she responded calmly to any situation.

"Don't you care what happens to Lauren?" she asked Isaak.

"Of *course*, I do. I can't believe you'd ask me that. She's just as much my sister as she is yours."

"The way you've been complaining for the past few weeks about this trip, I'm surprised you even care. Lauren is under a lot of pressure. The expectations are too much for one person. She may appear strong and sure of herself, but she's more fragile than she realizes," Chelsea lectured in a quiet voice.

I felt stunned. I couldn't believe they'd fought about me. We weren't in imminent danger, and I would never put my family in harm's way. The burden shouldn't be theirs. This only confirmed that what Quinn and I planned to do was right.

I stepped forward. "You guys, I have things under control. Don't do this."

Chelsea turned to me; her sympathetic blue eyes turned languid. I couldn't read what they attempted to convey.

"It shouldn't be this way. You've already had too many close encounters. We'll end this, Lauren. We'll find a way. You won't be alone." She reached for my hand.

My sister amazed me. I couldn't ask them to sacrifice everything. I couldn't be that selfish.

I turned resolute. This would end with me.

"So you see, *Isaak*, she needs us. She's not that strong."

"What? Are you saying I'd abandon her? She knows I'd be there for her if trouble came around. This is more than she can handle. I understand the situation quite well, *Chelsea*. We act as a family as we've always done. Why do you suddenly doubt my commitment?" Isaak reeled.

Chelsea wouldn't answer him.

"Are you two done yet?" Mom asked.

"We will now begin the boarding process for New Haven, Connecticut," a voice over the speaker announced.

"Here we go," Quinn encouraged in a light-hearted manner.

I looked over my shoulder to see Chelsea and Isaak facing in opposite directions, acting as if they were complete strangers. My parents followed quietly behind them.

We settled into our seats. Isaak slid next to Dad near the front of the plane. Mom and Chelsea sat in the exit rows, while Quinn and I continued to the back of the plane.

"I've never seen them attack each other like that and mean it, especially on my account," I said to Quinn in a low voice.

"They'll get over it. Don't concern yourself too much. They both probably needed to vent."

I sighed. "You're probably right. But I can't help wonder what Chelsea knows that she's keeping from us."

"I was thinking the same thing, too."

What could possibly cause my collected sister to become so worked up that she lashed out at Isaak? She never badgered anyone. The observer. And my parents hadn't questioned her behavior. I stared outside the window at the blue sky above the floating clouds as we reached maximum altitude. Fear permeated through the clouds.

My thoughts turned hazy, then empty. I jerked when Quinn elbowed me. Had it been a whole day? The captain's voice boomed over the loudspeaker as we descended into Philadelphia.

He gave us a brief description of the city—the birthplace of the nation. We inched closer to a body of water, a refuge surfaced where wildlife could have the chance to feed and grow on protected land. A good and secure place. I suddenly felt like one of its inhabitants, who needed sanctuary to ensure optimal survival of otherworldly invaders threatening to overtake my habitat.

I shook off the disturbing comparison. Isaak turned to me from the front of the plane with a reassuring grin.

"Chelsea and your mom are slowing down," Quinn said. We eased through the bustling crowd to the next gate.

"I'm going to stretch my legs. Who wants to get food?" Isaak asked.

"We'll go with Isaak and meet you at the gate," I told my parents. They left with Chelsea.

"Okay, what was *that* all about?" I drilled Isaak.

"Don't look at me. Obviously something is bothering her to the point that she's pretty worked up. I wish she'd fill me in on her recent discovery so that I wouldn't have to endure her heavy quips throughout this trip," Isaak complained. "It's not you."

"How can I *not* take it personally? It's because of me she's taking it out on you." We reached the sandwich shop. My energy to argue faded.

"Let her sort it out. I'm sure she'll tell you what's bothering her if you ask. But honestly, Lauren, I'm not bothered by Chelsea's attitude. This trip annoys me more.

I'm still not sure what we'll gain by going to Connecticut," Isaak said. He took a bite of his steak sandwich, mumbling in between chews. "It's no longer home."

Quinn and I looked at each other.

I drank some of the syrupy soda to get my thoughts off of Chelsea, but only reached another disturbing thought. Isaak's eyes widened and a 'what' expression formed on his face.

"Do you think we're being followed? I mean, I realize Mom was being cautious when she planned to have us sit apart on the plane, but do you honestly think we might run into something unexpected?"

Isaak gulped down his soda. "All the encounters with Mercedes and Nicholas and the strangers who seem to know you? Yeah, we should expect anything to happen. Don't you? I'd be surprised if we didn't have at least one visitor. You can't be crippled by the idea of a surprise visit."

Although I agreed with him, I felt uneasy. I wouldn't run, and I refused to allow self-doubt to cloud my better judgment. My powers needed to be at their best. *Don't fail me now.*

"I'm pretty much expecting anything. For everyone's sake, let's hope it's not everything all at once. I'm still learning how to overtake everyone."

"You know Mom and Dad are keeping tabs on Mercedes and Nicholas. If they decide to come out here, we'll at least have some notice," Isaak reminded us.

"Nothing brings me greater joy than having a *head's up* when I'm being stalked," I mumbled.

Isaak rolled his eyes. I was definitely in the running for the role of the next sister who would most annoy him. "It doesn't hurt. I know *I* would want forewarning. But if you'd rather we not tell you. . . ."

I raised my hand up to his face. "I'd rather know."

Quinn jumped to his feet and threw the empty wrappings away. He looked preoccupied. "Let's head out."

We weaved through the crowded passageways again, avoiding eye contact even as Quinn and Isaak drew in a few glances. I ignored them. It wasn't the random stares that tugged at me. Something else distracted me.

Quinn slowed down. "Lauren, what is it?"

"I don't know. Just a strange feeling," I muttered. I turned around to scan everyone nearby, but they all appeared to be rushing to their destinations. We slowed down again.

"I'm not sensing anything. Are you?" Isaak asked Quinn.

"Nothing unusual."

"What are you feeling, Lauren?" Isaak asked.

"Something is out of place . . . or someone." I carefully checked the surroundings in front of me and around me, but I found nothing unusual. "I can't pinpoint it."

The gate sign to New Haven loomed ahead. The rest of my family waited. Whatever had transpired, whatever feeling I'd had faded. Yet, omens felt real.

Discouragement swept over me. "It's gone. I can't feel it anymore."

Quinn looked uneasy. I heard his silent words, but then his demeanor abruptly changed.

Isaak grabbed my wrist. "Let's go."

I turned around one last time to see people moving through the bustling airport. Isaak's grip held firm. Time to leave *The City of Brotherly Love*.

2

NEW HAVEN

The short flight moved across my somnolent memory as I opened my eyes when the wheels touched down in New Haven. I never felt any rockiness from the commuter flight. Moisture clung to my body as we deplaned, and I was reminded of Chicago.

We reached the rental station. My parents requested separate vehicles, even suggesting a third one for Isaak and Chelsea. Isaak resisted.

"We'll meet you at the hotel," I said to them. They sped away in the dark SUV. I looked at my reliable and economic vehicle. Ordinary.

"I can't believe we're back here," Quinn muttered as we drove along the Connecticut Turnpike to the George Street hotel in downtown New Haven.

The city resembled the same one from a year ago when I'd visited with my family. I never felt captivated or shared a melancholic familiarity that my parents or Quinn had experienced. I belonged to the indifferent group with Chelsea and Isaak. This time, we would only spend a week out here, thanks to Isaak's negotiating skills.

"Does it bother you? I mean, the last time you were here,

you traveled to the present day looking for something you had lost," I asked Quinn.

"No, that's behind me. Just nostalgic for a different time. Besides, I found what went missing," Quinn said, squeezing my hand. "This isn't home any longer. Still, I can picture the old buildings and the horse-drawn carriages along the uneven roads. I can even hear the trains coming and going. We'd be approaching the Maxwell Inn anytime."

"Definitely not 1898," I replied.

"Absolutely 2012."

Downtown New Haven loomed within reach. I opened the window to allow the briny air and warm breeze to circulate inside the rental. The aroma differed from the crisp, fresh waters of Lake Michigan. Traffic slowed. Quinn glanced over his shoulder to where his family's hotel once stood, grand and impressive. He reached for my hand with a gentle grasp, which raised my guilt to a higher level. I kept my mouth shut to avoid disturbing his silent reflection on a hotel that had once been his home. Although the city had never felt significant to me, experiencing this moment with Quinn for the first time stirred something dormant that I couldn't explain.

I recognized some of the same shops and restaurants and saw new businesses that had opened up since the previous year.

"The hotel is coming up. We're so close to Yale this time."

"Ah, huh," he mumbled.

His thoughts lingered on another hotel, magnificent and resilient in its day before a mysterious fire had raged inside the marvelous place, bringing it down to only skeletal frames and floating ashes. It had changed the lives of the family who'd owned the hotel and left a faded memory in the footnotes of this city.

"I think the hotel would have lasted into this century," Quinn finally said.

"I'm sure the hotel would still be impressive today with you at its helm to secure its legacy. You'd have first hand experience of the original framework and functioning of the hotel. No one would know the difference," I said.

"If the fire had never happened, I would've placed a mandate on the hotel to retain as much original structure as possible. Modern technology would have to be incorporated around the place to not take away the hotel's character. I can see it already," he said. "If only, if only. . . ."

We pulled up in front of the renovated hotel in downtown New Haven. The concierge staff took the luggage except for the carry-on bags that Quinn and I kept. We followed them into the lobby where my family waited.

"Isaak made sure we'd get here before you did," Chelsea remarked and smiled. A truce seemed to have formed between them.

"Lauren, we've already checked in. Here are your key cards," Mom said as she handed them to me. "Let's relax for a bit, then we'll meet in the lobby at five thirty before going for dinner."

"Where are we going?" I asked.

"We'll let you know when we meet down here," Dad responded.

My family headed for the elevator.

Even dinner needed to be a surprise. The whole trip would be filled with last minute destinations and quick changes. I'd come prepared.

Quinn checked every detail of the hotel. I could see the

comparisons and the ideas going through his vibrant mind. "The color scheme suits the location. Shades of brown, cocoa, and cream seems appropriate next to the Ivy League school, keeping a formal, yet modern touch with the academic theme. The trim softens the place so you don't feel like you're completely in school," Quinn commented. "The wood construction looks solid, but I don't know about the floor plan."

"I don't think many students stay here unless they had family visiting for a special occasion. I'm sure there are less expensive places around campus. But I'm glad my parents didn't hold out," I replied.

"What other places did they have in mind? You never said what we'd be doing."

"I know we won't be in New Haven the whole time. And I'm sure we'll be in Bridgeport at some point."

Quinn took a final look around. Then, he said, "It might make it easier for us and for them if we didn't have anything set."

"Do you think so?"

"I'm sure we'll go to your parents' home in New Haven. I'd like to see it again with you this time, maybe get a different perspective. I haven't been there since I crossed over."

"I'd like that. Maybe then I'll remember something."

A false sense of nostalgia invaded my thoughts. I had lived here more than a century ago. What was I like? How had I behaved? Would I be the same person? Images circulated more vividly in my mind.

"I can see my parents' home—with clarity—and now I have reason to picture myself there. It's one of the reasons why we come here every year, so that I might remember."

"For better or for worse."

"Right. Even if the memories might not be so pleasant." My mind flashed through personal scenes before the turn of the century. The excitement and the sudden hesitation won me over. I wanted to be a complete person again.

Quinn looked at me strangely. Frown lines formed across his congeal face. "Don't even think about it."

"What are you talking about?" I asked, waking from my buried thoughts.

"You know what I'm talking about," he repeated. He propped up his luggage.

"About the memories?"

"No. Do I have to spell it out?"

"Yes, please tell me what's bothering you."

"This isn't a joking matter, Lauren."

"Who's joking?"

"Not a good idea, Lauren."

"You lost me."

"Okay. You want to go there. You want to go to Raefield's place and see for yourself what mystical or magical aura might be waiting in hopes that it would trigger some memory in your obviously dormant state."

"And what's wrong with trying to unlock the amnesia I apparently have?"

"You don't know what forces are surrounding the place. It could be a trap."

"It didn't bother you to venture into his domain when you first came here."

"That's different. I was very careful. I can sense another. And I didn't stay very long."

"And you don't think that I can be careful? Remember, I'm supposed to be stronger."

"That's not my point," Quinn said calmly. "I'm not tied to him. I'm not the one he wants at all cost. His connection to you might be strong enough to pull you in. His powers could be influential even if time has placed a distance between the two of you. The house is just bait. Once inside, his control might suck you in, make you weaker. We don't know what dark magic still lurks inside his estate. I'm not going to take that chance. Your family won't allow it."

"Leave them out of this! I can take care of myself."

"Not a chance!" His gray eyes turned stormy.

I met his glare. I looked deep and hard and found nothing but solid steel. I let out a defeated sigh. Hope diminished. The chance to finally know what had been taken from me moved beyond my reach.

"Wouldn't you want to know? Wouldn't you want to bring that missing part of you together to form a whole person? Everything could finally make sense."

Quinn stiffened.

"I would want to know. I would want to remember. Then, I could finally let go of what felt broken inside and move forward."

Quinn ran his hand through his wavy hair. He appeared conflicted. The guilt ate at him. He knew it wasn't right that I should be left at a disadvantage.

Defeat neared.

"The answer is still no."

"*Fine.* Have it your way . . . for now." I grabbed my luggage and stomped toward the elevator. Quinn followed slowly. We stood side by side at the elevator door in silence.

"I don't need a savior."

"I'm not looking to be anybody's savior. And I'm not trying to keep you from remembering. It's just not a good idea to go there. That's all."

I didn't respond.

"Don't be angry. We're here. We'll go to your parents' house, and we'll go to all the places that you've been to. Something is bound to trigger your memory."

I smirked. He tried to put his arm around my shoulder, but I pulled away.

"Okay, have it your way." Quinn moved to the other side of the elevator. We rode up in silence.

The elevator took us to the top floor where my parents had reserved three separate rooms. Quiet opulence and formality surrounded us. I searched for the rooftop exit.

"We shouldn't need it . . . yet," Quinn said.

"Just being prepared."

Quinn nodded. His gaze turned elsewhere.

"I'm tired. I just want to sleep," I mumbled.

"Sounds like a good idea," Quinn said, his eyes still fixed on the oversized room down the hallway. "I wonder what the presidential suite looks like inside."

"Maybe you can ask for a tour if it's not occupied."

"Is that sarcasm I'm hearing?"

"No, it's my sleepy head calling out her final words before collapsing."

I opened the door to a very clean and earthy room— cream, tan, and brown with Roman blinds covering the tall windows that were pulled down a quarter of the way to not obstruct the view. The city's skyline shimmered beyond the window. A definite old-world view of a city from yesterday-turned-modern appeared before us. I had once been a part of that world. I was determined to reconnect to her. For now, collapsing on the bed came first.

"Nice room."

"Yeah," I mumbled into the linen.

"We should get that nap before meeting your family."

I turned onto my back. "I'm surprised my parents chose a room with only one bed. They must really trust me." I gave him a wry smile.

"A *king size* bed I might add. If it makes you feel any better, I can push you to the other side."

"No, that's not necessary. I don't want the distance."

"*Now* she wants to be close." Quinn jokingly pushed me away. "Go to sleep."

"Already there," I yawned, pulling myself under the Egyptian cotton sheets.

If Quinn said anything, I became oblivious. The silence overcame the humming of the cars and the voices carrying over from the outside world. I don't know how long it took me to fall into a state of altered consciousness, because everything became still, and my thoughts fell into a sinking hole.

"*Lauren, Lauren. I need your help.*"

I abruptly shot up from my bed. "Who's in here?"

Silence echoed around me. I knew I wasn't dreaming. Just hazy.

"*Lauren, I'm here!*"

I jumped out of bed and scanned the dark room for the voice I heard calling me. The sun seemed faded behind the drawn blinds. "What do you want with me?"

No one answered. Quinn was gone. He hadn't awakened me to join my family. I glanced at my clothes. The same ones I'd worn on the flight.

"*Lauren . . . hurry!*" the voice urged. It lingered in the air around me until I heard a whimpering noise in the background.

"Wait for me!"

"Over here, Lauren."

I looked at the door. No one. But I knew the voice. It was no stranger to me. My own voice called out to me to lure me to a place it wanted me to go. I quickly grabbed my sandals and rushed out the door.

"Lauren."

"Where are you?"

I turned my head to the echo of my own voice down the narrow hallway by the suite situated in the far corner that had caught Quinn's attention earlier in the day. The hallway turned dark. Why were the lights dimmed and the shades pulled down on the grand windows? Something wasn't right.

Something shimmered. Light. I saw blue and white lights flashing under the door of the suite. My attention peaked. Too enticing.

Where were the warning signs?

Nothing.

It didn't matter. I told myself I needed to follow the light.

The light turned brighter, now sapphire and sky blue. Under the door, a mist emerged, a vaporish white haze, dancing around the entryway like smoke-filled air to warn me that something lingered behind the door. I hesitated at the entryway.

I'm supposed to go, I told myself.

"Hurry, Lauren! There isn't much time."

"Don't go!" I called out.

I quickly opened the door to a blinding light in its full grandeur—blue and dense. I managed to stay focused and searched for the voice. Nothing. The vapors continued to circle, then cocooned me.

"Where are you?" I pleaded.

My eyes stung and watered. The air smelled toxic. The

fumes from chemicals burned my nose. I searched for an opening to find clean air. Everything seemed covered by a dense layer. My chest began to hurt; it felt tight. I couldn't catch my breath. I gasped and coughed. Feeling weak. My mind turned hazy.

"Fight it, Lauren."

I was slipping. I couldn't fight the mist. Too strong. My legs loosened, and I began to fall. The mist would take me tonight before I could say my goodbyes.

"*Lauren.*"

A different voice emerged. Where had I heard that voice? I struggled for clarity as the mist continued to engulf me.

"*Don't go.*"

Yes! It was the same voice I had heard that first night in my room when an image appeared. The same voice that called me when—

"*Lauren, come back!*" Quinn shouted.

I struggled harder to free myself. I couldn't escape.

"*Quinn, it's trapping me!*"

"Lauren, snap out of it!"

"*Quinn . . . Wait for me!*" I suddenly opened up my eyes. My arms reached out into the air. Quinn stared back at me.

"You're here. You heard me."

"Of course, I heard you. I never left. You called out," he replied.

I sat up in bed. I just stared at him, then at the room. Everything remained the same.

"Who were you talking to?" he asked.

"I . . . I don't know. I was out there," I said, pointing to the door. "It was real. Someone called me to that room."

"What room? *Who* called you?"

"I don't know who. It sounded like my voice, calling me

out of this room. It wanted me to go to the suite down the hallway."

Quinn shook his head. "Tell me everything. Did you see anyone?" he asked.

"No. No one."

Quinn stepped away.

"That couldn't have been a dream. We don't dream. It was something stronger."

"No dreams," he replied.

"It felt so real, not like what I imagined a dream to be. I was in this room, but it was darker. The shades were drawn, and the sun seemed to be setting." I looked out the window and saw the late afternoon sun. "You were gone."

Quinn frowned. "I've been here this whole time."

I stared at the doorway. I remembered feeling the doorknob and hearing the door close. I envisioned the hallway again, which seemed unusually dark for a hotel. The room—it felt too real. All of the intoxicating vapors sucked me inside its trap, lured by my own calling. Then, I realized something was off.

"No, it wasn't real. Everything is out of place. The timing wasn't right."

I recapped every detail of my unearthly walk to the other room. This time, fear no longer existed.

"It sounded as if you were summoned. Or, if this doesn't sound too crazy, you may have undergone an out of body experience."

"Crazy . . . strange . . . mystical, that seems to be the norm lately. Tell me something useful. Who summoned me? Why? An out of body experience? Great, now I'm walking amongst the dead in my sleep." I jumped out of bed and rummaged through my suitcase for new clothes to wear.

"I don't know that much about it except for what Dr. Sendal has told me, but unfortunately, he's not here to give us an explanation. I'm sure your parents have some ideas."

I left the bathroom door ajar so that I could hear him speak. I splashed cold water on my face. I welcomed the simple realness of the water.

"It's funny how you mentioned the sky went darker and the shades were pulled in the hallway. If I didn't know any better, it almost hinted of foreshadow," Quinn said. "Lauren, do you know something I don't know?"

I brushed the snarls out of my hair. "Nothing you haven't told me that couldn't happen to any of us."

Quinn opened the door. "Come on, Lauren. I'm serious. Don't hold anything back. You know you're the most likely choice."

"No, the voice didn't tell me anything but to follow. After that, you called out to me."

Quinn looked satisfied for the moment. "If I hadn't heard you, I wonder if, hypothetically, you would've been stuck in the mist or mentally taken somewhere. Because in my only experience through the great mist, I don't remember it burning my eyes like you mentioned."

"Then I don't know what it's supposed to mean." I threw a few items into my purse. "Now finish telling me what you know."

Quinn looked at the alarm clock. "I'll keep it brief." He sat down on the bed again. "Some people, obviously someone like you, have the ability to step outside of yourself during those altered states of awareness, and only during that time."

"Sleep, I get it. Continue."

"From what I've been told, it's also through another force

which allows you to separate from yourself while you're sleeping. Something, or maybe someone, summons you. The reason why this happens, I'm not sure."

I thought about his explanation. It didn't surprise me that another supernatural event hovered at my door. "Could this benefit me, as in give me some insight, or is this meant to harm me?"

"That, I don't know. Let's side with benefitting you. I was comparing the visions you had about your birth mother to this."

"It happened during a major headache, and I was always awake. I just took myself elsewhere. It was the rock giving me those visions. This was something else."

"I agree. And since we don't dream, my only explanation for what happened to you—separating yourself in your sleep—is another force acting upon or manipulating you. Whatever great energy exists around you, something is attracted to it. Maybe the rock is even tied to it."

I grabbed a light sweater. "Whatever happens next, I must be ready."

"I don't think you can fully prepare. All the unknowns coming at us—at you—can't be handled on a whim, and clearly not by trial and error. It's too much."

"We don't have much choice. Whether it's me or this place or all of us, it's around us."

Quinn became quiet. I knew he couldn't disagree.

I looked at the lighted sky. "The city is waiting. Let's go meet them." I grabbed my purse, closing the door for the first time today in real time.

3

STORIES

Chapel Street buzzed with life, retail stores, restaurants, bars, and cafes open to the curious and restless public. It felt good to be out in the open and carefree, even if that made us more exposed. The Reed and Maxwell train marched along the street with Chelsea and I at the rear.

"I can't believe you had one of those. I remember Mom telling us about people having out of body experiences. She's actually seen a few. Not many are called to that level of self separation," Chelsea said in a low voice. "Some didn't even have a rock."

"I guess that answers my question if a person needed a stone. Did she say who?"

Chelsea took a few careful steps along the uneven sidewalk. She avoided stepping over any broken edges with her heels. "There was someone in her village. She witnessed an event at a local hospital where she trained as a nurse. Mom said the girl had powers beyond her years, but she didn't have a stone."

"She was a nurse?"

"Yes, something like that before she got married. It was 1873. She was an adult at age sixteen. There weren't many options for women in those days, and Mom knew she wanted to do something with her life. She didn't want to work for the family business, and she didn't want to be a housewife to a man her parents thought suitable for her. Anyway, nursing schools were just becoming established at that time. Her parents didn't want her going to Boston, living away from familiar people. So, she stayed in Bridgeport and trained on the job. She wanted to help people."

"I never knew that about her. I've only known about her careers in the present day, and after she told me where she really came from, I only knew that she taught school *in the past.*"

"Well, it was short-lived. She obviously didn't stay in nursing." Chelsea lowered her voice even more and slowed down to create a greater distance between the rest of the family and us. "While at the infirmary, she witnessed an event similar to yours by a village girl, who didn't realize she had split off from herself. Both sensed the other person's special abilities. Naturally, when Mom noticed the girl moving around and talking in her sleep, she knew it wasn't a dream. The girl later confessed to being called out by an uncontrollable force."

Every word Chelsea uttered stayed with me. "Who was she?"

"Mom wasn't there long enough to find out. The girl decided to leave the hospital."

"What happened to Mom?"

Chelsea stopped talking.

"Tell me what she told you."

"All right. But it's still a mystery to this day. Don't read anything into it."

"*Chelsea.*"

"You're probably wondering how a witch ended up in the hospital."

"It crossed my mind."

"Apparently, she had been doing a lot of magic, wearing herself thin and mixing with the wrong people. She was dehydrated, her wounds healing slowly."

Flesh wounds. I knew all too well.

"She confided in Mom about these powerful people, who lived in the outskirts of town, and how they wanted her to join them. When she resisted, they attacked her."

The busy bees swarmed around their prey, waiting for the victim to make a wrong move. The colony needed to grow. It would benefit the hive to enlist additional workers. I felt sad for a girl I didn't know, someone already alone in the world.

"Several days after she left, the girl returned to the hospital in dire condition. She was terribly weak. She appeared to have internal injuries. Mom tried to give her some special medicine to ease the pain and to aid in the healing, but the girl resisted. She didn't want to be saved. She knew it was too late for her. Before she died, she told Mom about the visitor who'd called upon her. The girl called her a spirit of the dead. The spirit warned her that within the hospital walls, many witches had died there in vain in order to seek some form of retribution by passing through the near dead. It didn't work, however."

I stared at a reflection of Chelsea and I as we passed by a window. "The girl was different, and so was Mom," I said.

"She warned Mom to stay away, to leave the hospital. Mom listened to the dying girl and did exactly as she instructed. She never returned."

I sighed. "What happened to the girl and her family? What about the outsiders?'

"The girl was parentless. Mom thinks the girl's father left after finding out she was a witch. Her mother passed away when she was a child. The girl was passed from family to family, and then to strangers."

"How sad."

"The outsiders were chased out of town by the villagers, who feared and demonized witches. The paranoia was rampant in New England at that time."

I looked up to see if Isaak or Quinn heard our conversation. They seemed to have forgotten we were even present.

"You mentioned another person having an out of body experience. Who was it?"

Chelsea looked straight ahead. "Your father."

"My *birth* fa—"

"Are you two coming along?" Mom asked. She had stopped walking and stood in front of us without either one of us noticing. "If I didn't know any better, I'd say you were deep in conversation about the rest of the trip. We have so many places to go."

"I know where *I'd* like to go," I remarked.

Mom studied me with troubled eyes. A reflection suddenly appeared in her swirling, hazel eyes. Doubt shimmered in those reflections, cautioning me to stay away for my own good. I wanted to reassure her, tell her not to worry. I could take care of myself. And then, the image vanished.

Mom turned away, and mumbled, "You're so much like your father."

Quinn and Isaak slowed their pace. "I think we should stop in there." Isaak pointed to the coffee house with a stage for live music. Tonight's feature was jazz.

"The man has his good moments," Chelsea remarked.

"Nice. I just know how to make a decision," Isaak responded.

*

We took a cab back after the show. The music and atmosphere took my mind off the girl in the hospital and my unexpected body separation experience. That girl could be me someday, haunted by spirits that wouldn't leave me alone. The thought weighed heavily on me. Then again, I hadn't been left alone since I moved out of my parents' home.

"I want to stop at the front desk," Quinn said to us.

My parents already stood at the elevator door, waiting to go up to their room.

"Is this about the room?" Isaak asked.

"Yeah. It's been on my mind since Lauren had that experience."

"I'm curious, too," Chelsea spoke up. We stood patiently at the front desk, waiting for the clerk to get off the phone.

"Can I help you?" asked the hotel clerk.

"I was wondering if room 722 was occupied. I hear it's a very nice suite," Quinn inquired.

"The presidential suite? Let me take a look." He punched some keys on the computer. "Just as I thought, it's still available. It's one of our finest—two bedrooms—very spacious and plenty of amenities. There's a separate living room with a full-size sleeper for your guests. Would you like me to make a reservation?"

"No. We'll keep our rooms," Quinn said.

"Very well. Enjoy your night," the clerk responded.

I looked over at the elevator door where Chelsea and Isaak stood patiently for the door to open. I leaned over at

Quinn. "Do me a favor and go visit Isaak in his room. I want to talk to Chelsea."

"Didn't you already have your sisterly talk tonight?"

"Did you hear us?"

"No, I don't have that ability. It was obvious you were talking about something important. I thought you'd gotten everything out in the open."

"We didn't have enough time to cover the airport disagreement with my brother."

"Oh."

"It won't take long. I want to find out what was bothering her."

"Right."

In the elevator, I mumbled to Chelsea about wanting to get her opinion about my out of body experience and that Quinn wanted to see their room. She nodded.

Isaak and Quinn went in a separate direction. When Chelsea and I came closer to room 722, images of a swirling mist flashed into my mind. My name echoed in the air again, this time more quietly. My body ached, and I felt jolts of energy running down my legs. Even my fingertips felt the pinpricks. I slowed down.

"Lauren, are you coming?" Chelsea asked.

"Right behind you."

Leave me alone.

The transgression disappeared.

I opened the door to my room. "They're really nice rooms. Mom and Dad didn't spare any details."

Chelsea remained quiet. Her observant eyes scanned my room. I knew she replayed everything that had happened this afternoon, similar to a forensic specialist surveying a room to determine the last moments before death claimed a victim.

Her careful movements mentally preserved the scene.

I was still alive.

"It's late. What did you want to talk to me about?" She appeared distant.

"Nothing, really. Just more time to spend with you."

Chelsea's eyes moved downward. She ran her fingers along the quilted bed before sitting down at the head of the bed in a comfortable fashion. Her face relaxed. I saw the clear ocean in her eyes again. I settled down beside the only person who was truly my sister.

"You want to know why Isaak and I argued," Chelsea said in a flat, matter-of-fact tone.

"Yes, although you seem to be getting along again."

Chelsea sighed. "It's not certain."

"What's not certain? It's important enough if it bothers you. At this time, anything is relevant."

Chelsea appeared sad.

"What's so terrible you can't tell me?"

Chelsea took in a deep breath. "Lauren, I don't have all the details, just feelings. And they change. The situation is very fluid. Even Mom, Dad, and Isaak tell me it's too unclear. The feelings began to surface a few days before this trip. I don't know why I'm the only one having them."

I looked at her and through her for what she tried to tell me. "But your feelings do say something, otherwise it wouldn't be important. Otherwise, you wouldn't have them. Isaak knew something was wrong and that's why you fought."

Chelsea remained silent. I saw the thin mist clouding her light eyes. She fought back, holding on for her sake and mine. She didn't want to say it and make it known to be true. But I already knew.

"Something is going to happen to me. I might not make it. There's a good chance I might not survive."

I said the words out loud without flinching. Plain and simple, and out in the open so neither one of us would be tormented any longer with the thoughts arguing back and forth within our own heads, wondering if either one should mention something so forbidden. At some point, I might die before this is all over. *Die.* I mouthed the words Chelsea couldn't say. Somehow, I relieved her of the burden she carried. My uncertain destiny now had a perfunctory ending with a clearer picture of who would remain standing. That didn't include me. Yet, for a small and satisfactory moment, I felt peace. There would be closure, and in it as beautiful and as triumphant as I wish it would be, my time would come to an end.

"Don't say that," Chelsea whispered.

I was still caught in my morbid and glorious death, that it might bring the end of chaos for everyone around me.

"It won't help us if you're gone," Chelsea said. "Don't look at it as a means to an end that would improve the situation for the rest of us. It would only mean that somewhere along the way, we failed you."

I came down from my martyrdom. "But if you feel it around you, then it must be in the works. There has to be a reason for the strong feelings you're having," I said, treading carefully. "Then I should do what I can to make this better for everyone."

"*Are you crazy?*" Chelsea stated. "Stop this! Don't say those things as if they're nothing at all. You act as though you've been thinking about this for some time, and now you're accepting it like some obedient dog just because I'm having these feelings. This *isn't* a game, Lauren. And having your death proven that powers beyond me are fulfilled is *not* what anyone wants. Do you *really* want to die?"

"I was just think—"

"We would all be devastated if you're taken from us. And, it doesn't guarantee anyone is safe."

"I wasn't making this into a joke. I only wanted to give us hope, so that in the end, we'd be free. You and everyone I know from all the troubles that are connected to me. That's all. I'm not trying to cause anyone more pain."

Chelsea let out a heavy sigh. She rolled herself back into position against the headboard, her facial expression distant and weary.

The night weighed long and heavy. The knowledge of an impending death fell upon my sister to carry. The circumstances and the events leading up to my demise remained unknown. This was far from over. I wasn't ready to give in.

I jumped up from the bed. "Listen, it's late and we've had some serious things put out in the open. I don't know about you, but my eyes can barely stay open. I'm sure everyone's wondering what's taking us so long."

My sister opened her meditative eyes. "We'll do what we can. This is far from absolute."

"And what does Mom think?"

"She isn't saying much this time. Dad seemed to be more alarmed about my feelings than she is. Or, she's keeping it to herself, which isn't like her given the fact that she's the one who usually worries the most," Chelsea said. "I'll keep you posted, naturally, but I wouldn't bring it up to them just yet. Let them come to you. Of course, if anything changes on my part, you'll be the first to know."

Another issue gnawed on my mind. "Chelsea, do me a

favor and keep this between us. I don't want Quinn to know just yet."

Chelsea didn't respond.

"I don't like keeping anything from him, but he'll flip out if he knows about your premonitions."

"Are you sure?"

"Just do this for me. I'll handle telling Quinn when the time is right." I thought about my and Quinn's original plan to leave my family during this vacation. It was the only way to free them from the threats against me. Would Chelsea's uncertain feelings offset any plan in motion, or would they confirm a pre-ordained outcome?

She nodded her head. She reached for her designer purse and high heels. Even though we were both exhausted, Chelsea managed to give me a warm embrace. I felt optimistic. We were sisters, always and forever.

Chelsea escaped through the heavy door. Two clicks of the door and security surrounded me. I quickly dressed into my nightclothes. As I headed for the bathroom, a key card passed through the lock and an electronic beep sounded.

"Are you asleep?" Quinn asked.

"Just barely awake." I said, yawning. "Sorry it took so long. You know how it is with girls. Talk, talk, talk."

"There seems to be a lot of that going on."

I wasn't sure what he meant, but decided to let it go. The long and eventful day exhausted me.

Quinn climbed into bed after turning off the lights. The AC hummed quietly in the background. For now, every pressing issue could wait; tomorrow would soon be here. Quinn fell asleep right away. I climbed in next to him. He stirred and wrapped his arms around me. My thoughts returned to Chelsea. Surprisingly, I accepted her foreboding thoughts. I ran the back of my hand against the soft hairs of Quinn's arm; he stirred again. A wave of grief came over me.

Just fight, I thought to myself as the shadows hovered.

4

LIVING VICTORIAN

I found myself surprised at how long I had slept even when the bright sun blared in my face through the small opening of the curtains.

"How long have I been asleep?" I mumbled.

"It's almost 10:30. You've been out a long time. I didn't want to wake you," Quinn said. He looked up from his book. "A storm could've come through and you would've slept through it."

"That bad, huh? I needed it."

Quinn rose from the corner table. "We all ate breakfast. There's plenty here. I asked them to pack a little bit of everything for you. You can heat it up when you're ready."

"Oh, I'm ready. Energy food. I'm low."

Like a beggar who hasn't eaten in days, I piled large portions of food onto the sturdy paper plate. I heated the food in the microwave. In seconds, I dined eagerly on the bounty from the hotel's kitchen. I could hear my parents saying, "Try not to be obvious."

"Slow down before you choke," Quinn said, giving me a strange look.

"I can't help it. I thought I was being careful," I grumbled in between bites of food. "I don't know why I'm so hungry. I've been eating well. I feel more depleted than normal."

"Here, drink some water to wash it down so I know it's going somewhere." He handed me a fresh bottle of water. The questioning expression still lingered on his face.

I drank the whole bottle of water, satiating my thirst. I'd already eaten half the food on my plate, and I wasn't close to being full. Why couldn't I satisfy my hunger? My internal energy force still called out for more. I needed more. I craved more!

"Something isn't right," said Quinn. "I've never seen you eat so much in such a short period of time and still look hungry."

"I know what you mean. My hunger is so demanding. Without the food, I feel weak." I went back to shoveling the food into my mouth. Quinn handed me another bottle of water from the stocked mini fridge next to the coffee maker.

"You've slept well, and a good amount. You should've been replenished and only needed your normal amount of nutrition. Yet, you're eating like your life depends on it. Something's very different."

I looked down at the empty plate. I'd eaten enough for three meals. The hunger finally subsided. The energy surge now flowed evenly through my veins as was normal, pumping the thick fluid into my organs and out to the periphery to wake every cell in my body. I felt strong again.

Clarity found me. "It's this place. Being in this city is different this time."

He rose from his chair and sat next to me. Quinn carefully touched my face. "It would explain the strange events going on. There's something different about you. I don't know what it is exactly, but there's something pulling or controlling you more than usual. Let's not overreact until we know if this is a personal threat or an apparent warning to help you. We need to be extra careful here." Quinn withdrew his fingertips from my face.

"I know what you mean." I thought back to the negative forces surrounding Chelsea. "I'll be careful." I avoided making eye contact with him. I threw away the empty food containers, then washed my hands. The need to keep busy consumed me. I turned the TV on and flipped through the channels.

"I don't think this should change our original plans. In fact, it gives us more reason to go ahead with it. Don't you think?" Quinn said.

"Sure," I mumbled as I dug through my luggage for clothes to wear.

Quinn didn't respond at first. Then, he asked, "Lauren, what's bothering you?"

"Huh? Oh, just getting my things together. Mom didn't say what she had in mind for today. Did she mention it to you at breakfast?"

"She made some suggestions." Quinn moved closer to me. "Listen, Lauren, if there's something bothering you, you'd tell me . . . right? I mean, I'm not going to drive it out of you, but I may hassle you about it until you tell me what it is. You know it's important to me if there's something going on."

I looked up at his tense face. "I'd tell you. I'm just thinking about everything. The best course of action."

"Okay, but if there's—"

I placed a finger on his lips before he could say anything else. It just wasn't the right time. "It's this place. Obviously, there's a connection to me and this city and everything that's going on. For good reasons or not, it's affecting me. The energy is different."

"What do you mean? Are you sick?" Quinn moved closer to me.

"No, I'm not sick. It's the energy flow. It's different. It's moving more chaotically and in spurts. It's like there's confusion. There's the core force, or the main current, but there's another source coming in at different angles. Sometimes I feel overwhelmingly strong and other times, I'm completely low. I don't know how else to describe it," I explained. "Can you feel it?"

"No, everything is the same to me. I don't feel any differently, and I don't sense any disruption in the energy in and around me." Quinn shook his head. "I don't know. I don't like this. Anything that deviates from the norm isn't a good sign."

I chuckled. "The norm. There hasn't been anything *overly* normal about me since day one."

"You know what I mean."

"Fine. Let's just keep them as signs until we know more. Maybe it's a good sign that's helping me." I gathered my belongings and headed for the bathroom. "Mom will be calling. They're waiting for us."

My cell phone went off; Mom was on the other line. Quinn picked up the phone. I propped my ear to the door despite water flowing in the background. Quinn's voice sounded steady. I heard, "you're waiting for us" and "the museum". That told me enough to know where we'd be heading today.

I didn't waste anymore time. I applied sunscreen and a little bit of blush on my face, then threw some essentials into a bag. My hair remained wet.

"Okay, I'm ready. Let's get out of here before we never leave."

The TV distracted Quinn. "They're broadcasting the Cubs game."

I grabbed his arm and led him away. We rushed past the special room as my stomach tightened. Nothing moved within the room. I released a breath. The hallway appeared different today than a day ago. Quinn tugged at my arm. Soon, we stood downstairs with my waiting family in the lounge. Mom and Chelsea spoke inches apart in a quiet tone. Mom looked up when we approached them with understanding eyes.

"Was it a base hit?" Quinn asked Isaak.

"Not fast enough. The other guy was quick."

"Let's see how quickly you two notice when we're long gone," Chelsea teased.

"That's fine by me. I could easily stay here, make myself comfortable, and order something at the bar."

"Simple pleasures for simple minds. What a way to waste your vacation," she said.

"It sure beats going to the living morgue. I'd be happy to erase that one off my list," Isaak quipped.

Mom shot Isaak a strained look.

"I'm done watching," Quinn remarked, nudging Isaak toward the lobby entrance.

"Errr," Isaak muttered.

The Reed clan plus one made their way out of the hotel lobby without further commotion. That's what Mom wanted. Everyone knew the routine and the location by memory. This time, my feelings moved differently.

"I'm driving," Isaak said.

"We'll meet you there," Quinn responded.

I grabbed Isaak's arm before he got into the car. "You don't have to go. This doesn't involve you, and I don't want you to be forced into going on my behalf. I can go with Mom and Dad. You, too, Chelsea. You can stay. You guys have already done enough," I said, looking from Isaak to Chelsea.

"Relax, little sis. You're not going alone. Besides, I wouldn't dream of missing another impromptu moment where you might have another epiphany and some hidden message opens up. We'd have to hold you down after you go into convulsions, and duck when your sparkling green eyes shoot out blinding gamma rays. With all the energy in one room with Quinn added to the mix, we'd have enough fire power to blow up the city, maybe even the entire Eastern front."

"Funny. Real funny, Isaak," Chelsea remarked, hitting him on the arm.

"*Ow*, that actually hurt. You should control that strength of yours," Isaak responded, messaging his arm. "Can't anyone take a joke? You're all too serious."

"Can we go now?" Mom muttered from the back seat.

"Sure, sure," Isaak said. He looked serious this time. "Don't worry about it, Lauren. We wouldn't let you go alone. Just getting my point across."

"C'mon. Let's get into the car. I know a shortcut. We can be there before they arrive," Quinn said.

Leave it to Quinn to already have the city mapped out even though it had changed dramatically since he lived here, and since he'd stumbled upon present day New Haven after coming through the portal. His time here had been brief before he'd headed out west.

"What else did Isaak mean by having more energy in one place?" I asked, getting into the rented car.

"Your family believes with all of us together and the energy circumventing the place, it could be pulled in by people associated to you."

"Electromagnetic markers or just bait?"

"However you want to look at it."

"Quinn, that's not an option," I said as we sped away. "I'm not using anybody so that I can somehow bring to life a piece of my past. I won't have it."

Quinn remained quiet and focused on the road. The close-knit shops and buildings moved further away as we headed north, away from the heart of the city. He made a sharp right turn, which I didn't recognize as the route to the place I had been to many times on different occasions. I secretly wished we would go elsewhere instead of the living morgue.

"No one is going to be bait," Quinn muttered. "I have a good feeling we can generate more positive energy. It'll be fine," he said, taking his eyes off the road for a brief moment. "This'll be a good thing."

Good thing. I wanted perfect. "Positive energy. That's what concerns me. *All* that energy is going to attract attention."

"Let's just get there and check it out, see if we missed anything. Try not to look at it as some possible catastrophe. We'll be all right," Quinn assured me, squeezing my hand.

"I know. I wasn't trying to be dramatic. I just feel like. . . ."

"Like what?"

"Like being here has set off another force, some other entity. I don't know. I can't explain it just like I couldn't explain the other events." I took in a long, deep breath. "I have a strange feeling we're not alone."

Quinn let go of my hand. He eyes became fixed on the road as we approached the bend to the unforgotten place. The newly manicured lawn with the robust sugar maple tree and the seasonal blooming flowers in the front yard, along with the inviting, open porch, validated the city's efforts to keep the Queen Anne in pristine condition. The abundance of rainfall had kept the property fresh and alive—*living*—as Isaak called it. I could smell the life flowing around the Victorian home. Too much life.

Mom had said the original white oak tree, which prevailed over this home for years, had been taken down in the seventies after infestation and decay. She described the withering tree as "unable to hold onto an empty home". A great ash had been planted in its place, but survived only a decade before disease took it over, too. The city nearly opted to leave the lawn treeless until one final attempt with the sugar maple had been made. Today, it stood vibrant and strong.

"It looks as nice as it did last year. I can't see any differences so far," I said.

"Let's go inside. Your family should be here any time."

The towering, wrought iron fence stood solid and impressive. Time and thorough maintenance had not worn down its majestic presence. The gates welcomed us across to the other side.

I hesitated; my head turned back to the car. "Mom said we loved it here. It was a great home even though we didn't live here for long. We apparently spent many hours on the front porch, and we entertained numerous visitors. Everyone felt welcomed." A twinge of sadness crept inside of me.

Quinn reached out and clasped my hand. "I'm here this time.

We're seeing it together for the first time like we did before."

My heart moved outward in a velvety rhythm to his words. I started to squeeze his hand, but stopped abruptly. What should have been a bittersweet moment between us was interrupted by a clashing noise as the gate slammed shut. My head jerked to see who'd closed the door. We stood alone; not even the shadows lingered at the entryway. I felt a low breeze skimming along my ankles. Icy air. Quinn narrowed his eyes at the closed gate, and then he turned back to the front door, which gaped open.

"It's just the wind," I whispered.

No one greeted us at the door. I noticed a security guard meandering along the edge of the fence, his sack lunch in hand. He looked bored by the solitude. He enjoyed an easy job, something less demanding for an older man who probably had seen his share of regimented jobs in previous years. Now, he could enjoy my house as freely as I once had.

"It's how I remembered it when I came through to the present day. They've kept it intact. The minor changes would be unnoticeable to outsiders. Those who had lived here and spent time here would notice. It's missing intricate pieces," Quinn explained.

I understood his meaning. In seconds, my feet moved up the staircase of the living museum to the second floor. I stared at the door to my room from the top of the stairs. I understood my place in this home. My fingers traced the wooden rails and continued along the floral wallpaper. A small hope filled my thoughts that the home could be awakened. I looked at my door again. I knew in that moment what appeared different.

Just like the previous year, the four-poster bed covered by a cream and red floral embossed quilt and hand-sewn pillows remained untouched. A narrow dresser and standing mirror stood on one side of the room while a chaise occupied the arched windows, and a writing desk and a corner table completed the large room. Ample amount of light came through the tall leaded windows with the yellow curtains pulled back. Even the stained glass windows above the arched windows appeared extra bright today. I noticed the transformation of this room into a guest bedroom. Above the fireplace and at the corner table, I pictured the photos Quinn mentioned that had once sat out in the open. They were gone. I sat down on the chaise lounge to feel how I might have sat here alone in this room, reading a book in the afternoon or just gazing out the window.

"They're here," Quinn said, standing near the door.

"I know. They're coming up the drive."

I moved away from the perfect window. I hadn't heard them coming up the driveway or felt their energy; that would've been too easy. My gut feeling had told me when they were still some distance away.

Why was I so different from my own?

I quickly moved down the wide staircase to greet my family, who stood near the parlor. Quinn also joined us in the formal room.

"You found a shortcut. We'll have to take that road next time," Mom said.

"There's going to be a next time?" Isaak grumbled.

Mom turned to Isaak. I expected a frown or a glare, but her face softened. "Only if Lauren wants to. And maybe she doesn't need to anymore."

Dad moved away from the parlor and into the entryway that connected the other rooms. "They still keep it like it was yesterday."

"It's a relic," Isaak commented, following closely behind. "You can't find many homes decorated like this anymore. It's so gaudy." He scanned the walls and the ceiling. "Does the house know you're here?" he asked me.

"What?"

"I'm surprised you didn't feel anything."

"No, I haven't."

Isaak walked slowly through the Victorian home, observing the formal dining room before moving into the antique kitchen and then into the great room. I followed him like his shadow until we stood in the center of the room, beneath the extravagant chandelier. The grand room boasted rich colors, intricate decorations, and ornate furniture displayed in the central room of the house. Today, this would've been the living room or family room, minus the colorful decor.

"Are you sure about that? I think you might've ignored the signs."

I turned my back to him. The room felt warm even though the city had installed central air to protect the interior's integrity and to make it comfortable for its visitors. We were the only guests here today.

"They're just feelings."

"Feeling what?" Quinn suddenly asked.

"See if you can get Lauren to dig into that memory of hers. She's bound to find something in the abyss," Isaak commented. "The sooner we come up with something, the faster we can leave this place. It gives me the creeps. I don't know . . . something about this place . . . like it's alive. It knows we're here."

I let out a nervous laugh. Surely, Isaak was being delusional and sarcastic, as usual. Alive. How can a place be alive? Yet, I felt more awake than I wanted to believe. The rest of my family moved into the grand room as I stood still. Energy brushed up against me.

I jumped at the sensation. I wanted to escape the room.

"Can you see the detailing in the trim and around the fireplace and at the edges of the window? They don't make homes like this anymore with that much carved molding and detail. One would have to special order all of this custom decor," Mom pointed out.

"I could see becoming attached to this place. It's not as garish as you think a Queen Anne might be," Chelsea added.

"It's one of the finest in the city. The Victorian era was something else." Mom looked over at me. "Lauren, do you see something?"

"What? It's nothing."

"Well, you seem quite distracted."

"It's . . . everything here. There's a lot of extra energy floating around."

Everyone focused on me. I waited for Mom to say something alarming, but she didn't. Only Quinn frowned.

"I should go back to my room. Something I want to check over."

"Do you want me to go with you?" Quinn asked.

"No, I'll be fine. It's my old house. I need to look at it again."

"She'll be fine," Mom whispered to Quinn, clasping his arm to hold him back.

"I told you it's alive," Isaak commented. "Or something else is here."

I sped out of the room, not taking the route through the kitchen this time but under the wooden arch of the great room. I glided up the stairs toward the second floor to my bedroom, the door still wide open. To the right, the governess's room stood meticulously altered just like mine to resemble a guest room, fit for any important visitor. Since learning the truth, I've often thought about this woman who had lived in my house in the room next to me.

I scanned the room for items I might have missed. What exactly had brought me back here? I thought about all the items that had been removed from this room. I knew the photos had been taken away for a specific reason, the clothing, jewelry, and any remnants of me wiped clean.

My attention shifted to the conical shaped window that extended from the great room. Nothing stood by the chaise lounge or along the windowsill, but the energy felt stronger here. This room had summoned me from downstairs. I'd felt it deeply even as Isaak urged me to confess. I had denied my own feelings. I moved toward the window and looked outside. I scanned the back yard, the driveway with a carport at the side of the house, and then gazed over the vast rolling hills and trees of the property. The pond in the distance was noticeable from this point. Nothing out of the ordinary sprang out. Yet, I couldn't move. I didn't want to move.

What was I looking for?

I needed to know whom or what had called to me. Why had I been summoned to this room? Had I been the girl in the tower, hidden away from the world? Had I been left here in my kingdom of solitude as punishment?

No, I want to be free!

My inner calls remained unanswered. I felt stuck. I couldn't move away, anywhere, from this forsaken window.

Tell me! Why was I brought here?

In my own thoughts and in my moment of struggle, the answers jolted me. I looked outside again to see where the wind had blown across the prairie and over the trees and beyond the hills, the trees bent over in a uniformed line. The path became clear. I understood this time.

"Lauren, stay away."

I didn't want to listen to the voice. A new voice. Another voice. I knew what needed to be done.

"You brought me here and now I know. I can't leave it alone."

Silence.

I turned back to the wondrous and magical window. The energy moved beyond the lead glass and the picturesque window. This house symbolized a great part of me, of who I used to be. It also reminded me of all I had lost. It had fully awakened this time.

"Don't go."

"I have to. Then why did you tell me?" I asked, not turning away from the mesmerizing window.

Again, no response. I didn't care. Was she really helping me solve my problems, or was she creating new ones?

The wind picked up speed, and the clouds darkened at the horizon. The trees swayed and danced. Even the pond in the distance became turbulent. I thought rain would come down.

"Lauren, come away from the window," said a familiar voice in the background.

My thoughts suddenly cleared. I watched the wind vanish, then the stormy clouds disappeared. Everything settled again.

"Mom, I didn't hear you come in."

"I heard your voice. Whom were you talking to?"

"Just myself. Thinking out loud again."

She looked at me keenly. "You'll tell me if something or someone was calling you."

"Of course."

I didn't look at her. I couldn't hurt her in that way. What I saw couldn't be ignored. There was a reason for coming here. I needed to see it through. Then, I remembered the other arrangements Quinn and I made.

"We should go downstairs. Everything is nearly set."

I was puzzled. My family planned to come here, not just to jar my memory. I followed her with all the trust in the world. After all, she was my mother.

"Let's look at the other rooms before we begin," Mom said, leading the way down the wide stairs.

"What are you talking about?"

"It's time we go beyond these walls."

She led me through the double wood doors of the library, once my father's office. It was the first room on the left of the entrance hall past the front door. I had seen this room on a dozen occasions. Nothing appeared different from the earlier years. The same fine wood paneling and trim, the array of books on the shelves, and a simple chandelier suspended from the ceiling. I walked past the mahogany table, tracing the edges with my fingertips. My eyes shifted to the two small photos of my parents hanging on the wall. They looked so young and honorable. A small ache passed from my chest to my stomach.

"They were the best of people," Mom said. She took my hand and led me back into the entryway before my thoughts carried me away.

We walked near the stairway by a room I seldom remembered. The room had been simply made with a small bed and a few clothes in the armoire. A man had lived here, but he was no stranger. This had been the butler's quarters. I remembered Mom had said he'd lived with the family for twenty years, longer than the cherished nanny who looked after me in my childhood. He had been a trusted man who was handy around the home and who had been a part of the family. I wished I had known him, too.

We skipped the refined parlor. It was commonplace to have a formal meeting room in every Victorian home. Apparently, my father had used it for private business conversations, instead of the library when he had more than one guest visiting. We had convened in the parlor after Sunday dinner.

We entered the formal dining room with its rich sideboard and matching wood paneling. The enormous table sat ten people comfortably. A large mirror hung on one side of the wall, an elegant crystal chandelier suspended from the painted ceiling. The beautifully designed stained glass windows framed the double doors, which were reminiscent of the Victorian Age.

"Just remember everything you've seen so far. Keep the images alive," Mom said.

I did as she requested. I made mental pictures of everything I saw. I paid special attention to my bedroom and to the great room. Then my mind drifted to a room I desperately wanted to see. I envisioned standing at the towering door, ready to open the past and see what would be different this time.

"Not today," Mom said solemnly.

My parents' room had not been a focal point of this trip even with the circumstances surrounding their room—the blazing fire that supposedly started in their bedroom, ultimately killing my birth parents. I wished I had gone into their room before my family arrived.

We walked out of the polished dining room at the end of the long hall. Instead of walking through the antiquated kitchen and out onto the back terrace to enter the living room through more stained glass doors, we made a grand entrance through the archway of the great room. I suddenly felt as though time shifted from the present to the past. I turned my head to see the charcoal-colored cast iron stove in the kitchen that was built into the back wall and the copper pots hanging from the hooks. I imagined standing in the kitchen with my mother, the cook explaining to me the meal arrangements of the day. We stood around the wood table, preparing a full course meal. Then, just as quickly as the images appeared, they dispersed into fine mists into the crevices of the ebony stove. My attention turned back to the bright room in front of me, where my existing family stood patiently, waiting and wondering what I had just seen.

"Something catch your eye, Lauren?" Isaak asked.

"Oh, no. Just picturing what life would have been like."

"Or should I say you were seeing ghosts?"

Mom shot him a skeptical look. "You were definitely the mistress of the house, if not equal to your mother. There wasn't a room you stayed out of except for the employees' rooms. Even the library, which your father mainly used, had your signature on it."

"I'd agree with you on that one, Helen, except that she spent time visiting with the governess in her private chamber. I remember Lauren saying she and Clara were very close," Quinn added.

Finally. Another person. Clara.

A real person surfaced into the imaginary figure in my thoughts, someone who'd lived in my past and wasn't related to me, yet had known me as a child and as a young woman in the days of Victoria. How I longed to know her and remember her!

I looked up at everyone in front of me. Isaak cleared his throat and said, "Too bad you can't remember her, either. Anyone would be something. Well, except for Raefield."

"Yes, let's hope that's not her first memory into the other life," Chelsea commented.

My parents looked at each other. Then, Mom said, "Shall we begin? I think now is the right time."

"Well, I'm glad you're finally going to tell me what you've been planning. I was wondering if it was something everyone here had done before."

"Lauren, take my hand," Mom ordered.

"Finally, on to the good stuff. Might as well wake everyone up," Isaak muttered.

"Shhh. Can't you stop talking for one minute?" Chelsea scolded. "I want to concentrate."

"Oh, I forgot. You're a newww bee. And you call yourself a witch, a female dominant heretic."

"I was born with as much power as you. I don't use it to dissent with the masses. Besides, I've only done this in theory."

"Isaak, leave it alone," Dad muttered.

"Okay. I guess you haven't had any reason to use it."

"Lauren, stand across from me. Reach out and hold both of my hands. Your father will do the same and hold onto you and me." Dad came around and seized both of our wrists, his arms extended. We formed a T, Dad standing to my left.

"Now, Quinn, stand across from Oren and do the same thing. Grab Lauren's wrist and mine." Quinn did as instructed. We made an intersection—a plus sign—with all of our arms connecting to each other.

"Chelsea, come to the right of me and do the same. Grab Dad's wrist and mine," Mom directed. "Now, Isaak, stand to my left."

He moved in that direction. He stood to the left of Mom and to the right of Quinn. Everyone stood opposite me. We formed a human tree; I became the trunk.

"Hold on everyone," Mom ordered.

They held on tighter. A solid union sealed the bonds of my family line. We became bound and locked as blood and water might live synergistically in the same life pool. Something extraordinary surfaced.

"Whatever happens, don't let go," Mom instructed. Every hand gripped tighter around the other person's arm.

"Don't let go."

An echo of the same words drifted from the past as if they were spoken only yesterday.

"Lauren, I want you to concentrate on this formation. Pull all of your energy on us. We're the focal points, and you're here in your home in New Haven as it was when you lived here so many years ago. Take yourself to that place. Be her again."

I followed Mom's command without hesitation. I focused on this shatterproof link we formed so easily. Each branch securing each limb so that nothing could break the chain— the tree of knowledge.

It simmered. The quiet energy floated into the air and surrounded the magic tree. I felt a surge. I felt greater life. The pulsating rhythm flowed smoothly inside of me to awaken what had been dormant for so many years.

Mom closed her eyes. She chanted in some ancient language long believed to be lost.

"Paz de' tŭe. Paz de' tŭe. Ghäyam mali blèy äj sun whäzi comba rhè naelâ. Māza blèy rhån! Māza blèy rhån!"

Her lips moved to rhythmic words I didn't recognize. Over and over, she gave voice to the mysterious words in a foreign tongue. My father joined in the scripted words. Then Quinn, Chelsea, and Isaak repeated the chorus. When the power shifted, I turned the energy onto me and to a time during which I'd once lived.

The room gently quivered as if the earth awoke to the melodic calls coming from my family. The chandelier rattled, causing the crystals to play off each other like high-pitched bells. Time appeared to bend back and forth as light and darkness intermixed. The home knew us and understood we would bring it further to life. We held our embrace, because my life depended on their support.

"Uhhh!"

Quinn shot an anxious look at me before a power greater than him stunned the emotion away. He became transfixed.

The energy flowed forcefully through me and out into the great open for everyone to witness its magnificent command. It stunned me and raged within us before the next event. I scanned the room to see everyone in its control. Mom chanted louder.

The room shook and spun like a top out of control, yet nothing appeared to be crumbling into pieces. Soon. . . .

"Cross over now!" Mom yelled.

I let go of the room. I stepped away, at least in my mind. I don't know how I did it, I just did. My family faded into the background and into the listless air until I couldn't see the shadows of their faces. They released me, and I was alone. No, I let go. I walked away from them.

The room shifted but the differences were slight. I looked down at my wrists. A passing memory of their strong grip left my skin. No marks. I really was alone. The room appeared exactly like the present day, except when I looked closer, I noticed a blue patterned vase standing alone on a corner table that hadn't been in the previous room. My mind drifted to some fateful words from Emily Dickinson.

We never know we go,—when we are going
We jest and shut the door;
Fate following behind us bolts it,
And we accost no more.

I walked towards the vase, nearly tripping on the long, pale crimson pattern in front of me. My feet felt tight and conformed.

"Everything's as it should be," I mumbled.

I took small and dainty steps and shuffled my dress against the canary colored chaise just enough to hear the smooth fabric brush against the upholstered furniture. The clock struck 3:00 PM. I shuffled around the room back and forth like a stray animal while holding my skirt close to me, not knowing exactly where I wanted to go. The well-fitted white blouse with its puffed shoulders and sleeves seemed rather constricting during my need to break away. The glass double doors that led out to the stone terrace seemed like the perfect escape route, but my senses told me I needed to be close. I hid in the corner between the great room and the kitchen, because I desperately wanted to be here. Fear stayed with me at the same time.

"Let us convene into the living room today, instead of the parlor. The sun feels so warm on this surprisingly chilly day. You would think that autumn had opened her doors and told summer to leave," the woman said.

"I agree. It's rather strange to have this early cold front coming from the sea since we hath ourselves been severely burdened by nature's warmth," he replied.

I didn't recognize his voice, but I knew the sound of her sweet words that had been lost to me.

"Phillip should be home momentarily to join us. Or, if you wish to see him in the library on his arrival to discuss the important details that you have uncovered, that shall be of your choice. In the meantime, tell me about your recent acquisition. Does the motor churn?"

Cold air penetrated through me as a sign of the new season arriving earlier than expected. It pushed open the double glass doors that I'd conveniently left ajar. My heart quivered. This was a moment I'd dreamt of since my first memories. I couldn't escape without being seen nor could I move through the door, which led into the kitchen, without possibly running into a house servant. I didn't really want to escape, not yet anyways.

"My heavens! Did the wind do such a thing and blow the door open from the inside out? We *are* in for a strong season," she remarked, coming toward the glass door.

I stood motionless as each shallow breath expelled while my heart raced like a stallion running to the finish line. *Thump, thump. Thump, thump. Faster and faster, victory neared.* My stomach completed acrobatic turns and pulled at my organs; my skin tightened inside of my own cave until everything pushed upward against my inflated and pounding heart.

Her silky, ruffled dress sashayed ahead as she carefully took a step outside onto the stone terrace. I stared at the profile of the woman who haunted my visions. She looked straight ahead into the greenery; her eyes fixed on some image in the distance. She smiled. My mother stood eloquent and serene. Her dark, wavy hair was pulled back into a bun, reminiscent of her time. Then, her deep eyes scanned elsewhere in the landscape for anything unusual beyond the wind, which blew open my hideaway.

The wind came again, as forceful as before, and it blew against my skirt. She turned toward the corner where I stood and stared at my swelling eyes. I was caught. I froze with the victory prize that stood in front of me. My neck tightened; my throat dried up. Yet, I refused to make any whimpering sounds. My thoughts scrambled quickly with the words rehearsing in my mind, words that I'd wanted to say for so long.

She made no remark of surprise. She just stared at me with her beautiful face and understanding dark eyes until I could no longer contain the salty tears streaming down my face.

"Mother."

She moved closer, as if understanding my need to stand alone in this hidden corner. "I've been looking all over for you. Don't hide from me any longer," she muttered.

My arms longed to embrace her. *Mother! I've dreamt of this day for so long!* It would be the first time that I could remember, the first *real* time, all over again!

She stood inches away from me, from my overjoyed and long awaited embrace. The turmoil would be over. I could now find a sense of peace, knowing I would feel the realness that my mother truly existed in my life. My breathing sounded labored.

Then she walked past me, her eyes observing something again in the distance as I reached out to her. She stared in that direction for a few more moments before reaching for the door that led into the kitchen.

"Mother, I'm here. *Look* at me," I cried out.

She placed a hand on the door and stopped for a moment. "Be careful," she whispered.

She then grabbed the doorknob, checking to see if it remained closed. Satisfied, she breezed past me, and back into the great room through the glass door.

I lowered my head in defeat.

5

THE UNINVITED GUEST

A significant amount of time passed after I dissected everything that had just transpired. Her lovely face, the proper gown she wore, and the indifference in her expression as she stood in my very presence. A chill ran through me. *My mother stood right in front of me!* Anger and coldness seeped in.

Just breathe, Lauren.

Then, numbness and grief took over, each finding a place at the core of my existence. I'd lost her again, despite being given this monumental opportunity to reunite with her in this life.

Momma, why can't you see me?

In those few moments that changed my world, I darted through the glass door before she could shut me out completely. The howling wind struck the translucent door again. I thought the wind would leave a horrific mark against the pane or cause the antique glass to shatter, but the door held firm. I would do the same and stand in her presence again.

"Where did he go?" she remarked aloud. She briefly looked around the great room before casting her eyes through the arched entrance that led into the main hallway.

"Mom, it's me, Lauren. Don't go. I have so many things to ask you."

She stood there for a moment, her back to me, and waited as if something had finally caught her senses. This time, just maybe, she'd heard me. I was finally reaching her.

My mother said something inaudible and walked under the arched opening, leaving me alone again with my sinking heart.

The room and the whole house felt uncomfortably still, despite people moving from room to room in this large dwelling. The puttering noise of my failing heart left haunting footsteps to remind me of what used to be. I felt emotionally drained. I wasn't sure if I could take it any longer.

"Will it always be this way?"

No. I refused to let myself slip away. I knew in the deepest of my thoughts this would happen. I was just here . . . figuratively.

"I wasn't sure if you left or took leave into the library to wait for Phillip. I had not heard the carriage pull forward, so naturally neither you nor Phillip were in route. Is the air too drafty? I could ask Nathan to start a fire."

The same man came toward me from under the archway. "No, I'm comfortable. I'm eager to speak with your husband," the man replied. He walked through the shadows and appeared in full view with the sun shining into the grand room. I knew at this moment why I couldn't keep my eyes away from him.

Raefield.

"Well, let us have afternoon tea here, and we shall await my husband's return. I'm sure he's just as eager to hear of your news, or what you've been told. We must keep our senses open and forgo any hasty action."

"Faye, I couldn't agree with you more. The less people aroused and involved, the better."

They moved toward the elegant floral sofa that balanced out the bright yellow chaise. I stood far enough away at a safe distance to observe everything being said and done. I knew they couldn't feel my presence, yet I found solace standing apart from them. I couldn't unravel again, knowing my mother didn't know I existed.

"We must remember our place if we are to be held to a higher standard. The general public has had their fears provoked and tested, and even exaggerated to the point of unnecessary hostility. As mayor, Phillip is doing all he can to bring balance to the city to avoid hysteria as we've seen in some of the East coast cities."

The striking man nodded. I caught myself still gazing upon his face in awe. There was something so appealing and regal about this man. Was it his mesmerizing green eyes and albino features, or the way in which he put his hand on my mother's hand to reassure her that my parents were supported in their efforts? His angelic face projected comfort and understanding. A trustworthy demeanor exuded from Raefield, a person who could win the hearts and minds of those around him. This face belonged to the person I despised. It was difficult to look away and not be drawn in by his nature. I turned away in shame.

"Raef, we knew we could count on you to support us in this cause. We *can* exist with the other humans. We've been successful in many places. We have to win them over. Our home is here as it has been for centuries, for time longer than recorded," she said, her voice fading.

"You know, Faye, I am in full agreement. Two worlds can cohabit peacefully. I've seen it done. However, if Phillip and the other members decide to bring about this change, you have my unwavering support."

My mother looked pleased. She'd found a true ally in the eyes of her worst enemy, but she still didn't know his real motive. I shuddered at the outcome, which had led me here today. Still, my desire to know the events before their deaths kept me focused. My only concern, the time limitation before the spell would call me home.

"We are still to practice caution and discretion. Very few people outside of the order are aware of our existence, and we'd like to remain as such," my mother said.

"I understand your thoughts. Of course, that would be most practical."

They turned to the woman walking into the room, carrying the afternoon tea. Her eyes looked familiar to me, but I couldn't place her face in my memory. She exuded warmth.

"Clara, where is Vera?" my mother asked.

"I've sent the woman home early, ma'am. She was no longer needed as you and Mayor De Boers will be dining out this evening. Nathan has gone ahead and arranged for the carriage to take you into town at six this evening. It would be wise to carry a heavier coat in this unforeseen chill we're experiencing." She placed the tray upon the table. "Mr. Raefield," she said warmly. "How good to see you again."

"Clara, you know to call me Raef."

Clara beamed.

"You always plan ahead, and I thank you for the dedication to this family, Clara. We've been blessed to have you in our home."

"It's my honor," she said, pouring the hot tea into the porcelain cups. I wondered if the tea contained the family's enhancement recipe. They sipped the warm drink, which looked enticing.

"With your daughter being a grown woman, my assistance to her is hardly needed. She seems to take on the role naturally, and with a role model such as yourself, who could ask for a superior example. There is nothing new to teach her that her rapid mind could not absorb. Has she decided to further her studies?"

My mother sighed. "She's grown up too quickly for her mother."

My stomach did a few twists. *Mom, I wish for many things.*

"Clara, as long as you're in my home and your services are needed, whether as my personal assistant or liaison, you have a place here with us. You and Nathan have been a godsend!" My mother turned her head away toward the entrance in response to the noise coming from down the hall. "He's home."

Oh, Father. I've waited so long to see you both.

"Nathan, where has everyone gone to?" my father asked from the entry hall.

"Phillip, dear, we're here. Look who has come by to see you?"

"Ah, Raefield, good man. I expected you this day. Work keeps me busy these past few weeks, but the reward is good. A visit from you is always welcomed," my father said, giving this angelic man a brief embrace.

I watched how my father looked adoringly at this man as my mother had done like a soul that could be trusted with the family jewels. I was tempted to reach for his neck.

"If there isn't anything further, I will take my leave and

join my sister this evening at her home. They will send a carriage for me," Clara announced. "It's good to see you again, Raefield. Mr. De Boers, Mrs. De Boers."

"Have a fine evening, my dear," my mother replied.

My father found a seat in the luxurious armchair next to the sofa with a cup of tea in his hand. His eyes resembled his sister's except his were a brighter hazel, and the chestnut contours of his hair reminded me of Isaak's. I looked at my own straight hair and wondered where the waves had gone. I ached to know my father again.

"What a strange day this has been!" Mom remarked, seeing the wind crashing against the elegant windows. "Here, you see the sun so bright and so calm today, yet within the hour a storm is surfacing." She cautiously turned to my father. "Are we expecting anything?"

"I'm not aware of any news."

"Nor I, Faye. It has been quiet," Raefield replied. He looked deep in thought for a moment before turning to my parents. "Your help . . . are they to be trusted? They are, after all, regular humans."

"Oh, Nathan and Clara have been with us for some time. Surely, you can sense their loyalty after meeting them on a dozen occasions. Nathan is more than a butler. He's a steward, if you will. He oversees the daily activities and functions of our home under my advisement. And Clara, she has been with us since Eden was very young," my mother said.

Eden.

"They gave you a lovely name."

Oh, Quinn. You were always holding on. I couldn't help but feel guilty and sadness for him when I think about the first time we had spoken at the coffeehouse. Was I a disappointment from the girl he had known, had searched for, for two years? He had expected someone else. This Eden, who no longer existed, transformed into me. I buried that unpleasant thought.

I hadn't realized what was happening from my own deep thoughts of Eden that when I looked up at the people in front of me; there, Raefield stared directly at me.

No, it can't be. He can't see me. None of them can. I instantly froze.

"I guess you're right, Faye. I'm sure they're loyal to your family, if by now you would've suspected disloyalty," Raefield remarked flatly.

"Let us move on to more pressing topics. Raef, I'm aware you have some news to share with me. Shall we continue this newsworthy conversation in the library so that I can show you some documents that have come to my attention?" my father suggested.

"I will join you momentarily. I want to bask in the sun's rays for a few moments longer before convening in that somber den."

My father chuckled. "Enjoy the rays." He and my mother walked out of the room, abandoning me here as my fears grew.

Raefield kept his stark green eyes directly at me. They narrowed. He scanned the air where I stood.

I turned into stone.

"*Spirit*, why have you come?" he hissed.

I said nothing. I held still. Even the trembling muscles that wanted to contract wouldn't dare move. I tightened my lips and clamped down on any accessory muscles from aiding my lungs to fill with air. Nothing would escape me.

How did he know?

He began to walk around me, his determined eyes never leaving the personal space that surrounded me. "*What* do you seek? I have not called upon thee. Your presence is not welcomed!" he hissed even louder.

Still, I said nothing. His angelic face vanished completely, replaced by a snarl I knew to be the true Raefield so cleverly disguised. My safety felt imperiled.

Raefield stopped his dizzying pace and reached into the air. I took in a quiet, deep breath and wished for my powers to find me in this form. At this moment, I desperately needed those powers. His hand and his arm went through me without disruption. I felt nothing. I was the air. Again, he moved his arm back and forth, over and over into the space I occupied. He found nothing convincing. After a few moments, Raefield retreated. His glare and sharp, commanding eyes bore through me.

Something stirred within me. Something caught me off guard that I couldn't control any longer.

No, not yet!

A power surge charged ahead, causing me to react. "*Get out. Get. Out. Of. My. House.* **Leave my family alone!**" I took a step back, startled by the words that came out of my mouth.

The wind hissed and pounded at the windows. Raefield narrowed his eyes; he didn't intend to back down. Then his lips curled upward to form a crooked smile. "Another time, spirit." He turned his back to me, his demonic eyes fixed into my memory.

I let out a breath of relief. Caught. I could not afford to be careless when I'd come so far. My mind raced for an exit point before he discovered the spirit was actually me, not something he could conjure up. Everything would be compromised! The present moment, the future, *my family—me!*

How could I've been so naive?

"Raefield is very powerful. What Raefield wants, Raefield—"

Nicholas's words echoed as a clear warning in my mind. That was enough for me. If he could call upon a spirit of the underworld, he could achieve anything sinister. I turned around and headed for the French doors that led out onto the terrace. I didn't need an opening. In no time, I stood out on the stone terrace. How would I get back? How could I contact my living family?

I ran across the romantic lawn, through the English garden, and into the late summer blooms. My body remained in control. The shrubs and the bushes hissed. They whispered indescribable words as the pine needles rattled uncontrollably. The wind then took on a greater form, resembling a fierce storm closing in from a distance to flatten the land around me.

The mature trees called, *"Eden . . . Eden".* They swayed. They whipped through the air; their voices moved in a secret frenzy as I passed through their domain.

"RUN, EDEN, RUN! Get as far from here as possible. Keep going, Eden. Don't look back. Save Lauren!"

I did as commanded. I ran to the edge of the lawn, to the far corners of the estate. I searched everywhere for an escape route—some opening—to take me away from Raefield. I thought about my parents. If only they were real. At least I'd the chance to see them this one time. My thoughts returned to my escape. Would my living family be ready to take me back? I ran toward open lawn and collided midway. My hands pressed against an invisible wall. I couldn't move it. I pounded and kicked until I risked injury.

"*No!*"

I pressed my hands against the unbreakable wall and closed my eyes. The energy coursed through me, releasing through my hands. Light and heat fulminated.

Nothing.

Of course.

The house and everything surrounding this place belonged to the transformation. I remained stuck in my own trick, and Mom couldn't help me from the other side. Perhaps she did attempt to bring me back; I couldn't tell. Determined not to feel defeated, I slowly walked back to my home. What if I never returned? A hollow feeling moved through me.

I will get back.

The yard and the garden appeared more beautiful than I remembered; everything turned calm. The bright green leaves, the fresh cut grass, and the bountiful shrubs all lay out so peacefully and in harmony with the rich, summer flowers. Picture perfect and in pristine condition. I slowed down. My senses caught the sweet, fragrant air. I inhaled again. Something alive stirred within me.

"Think, Lauren."

I stopped to search and feel for any weakness in the invisible wall. I looked for signs here and from my family on the other side. Nothing emerged. Then, the shadows closed in, and I ceased to focus on going home.

Quinn.

He emerged from under the tall shrubs, stepping from the hidden foliage and out into the open where the sunlight shone upon him. He wore a white Faraday shirt and taupe Dodge City pants with black shoes of the day. He looked like the Quinn I knew.

"Where did she go?" he wondered aloud.

As Quinn walked past me, I reached for him. I knew all too well that it wouldn't make a difference. My heart sank for a moment, then I realized this illusion was history already played out. I remained a spectator. I watched Quinn move closer to the house. He paused several times and scanned the horizon. His eyes became fixed on an image that suddenly appeared from behind the mysterious walls of this Victorian home.

She appeared dressed like me, and I was dressed like her. The eyes reflected the same color as mine, hair done the same way, and a smile that I've seen a thousand times. We looked and moved and stood identical. Her face emitted freshness and glowed in the afternoon sun. Her eyes beamed with joy, her smile radiant and full of warmth for the man who stood before her. She looked happy. She represented the young, modern woman, ready to face the new world when it turned the corner into the next century. And so unaware of what lay ahead. . . .

"Eden, where have you been? I've looked everywhere for you. I spoke with the staff and talked to your family. Nobody could find you."

"And here I stand, right before you."

Quinn shook his head and laughed softly. He embraced the young woman, holding her tight, like she might easily slip away and become lost in another time.

Eden let go of him and reached for his face. "I'm here. What's the reason for your concern?" "I don't know. Something troubles me, like I'm going to lose you. It's just . . . something seems out of place."

"Shhh. Let's not imagine bad things. I'm not going anywhere without you."

I couldn't see Quinn's face, but she spoke the words he wanted to hear. He held her even tighter. Then, Quinn lifted her up off the ground and turned her around so that I could now see his relieved face. He tilted his head; our eyes met for the first time again.

I gasped. I took a step back. Could he feel and see me standing here, watching them? At first, he seemed confused. He said nothing, only stared in my direction. Then, his expression turned cloudy. I felt frightened, knowing what I represented—a figment from the future trying to warn them. I believed this shouldn't happen, yet this type of magic possessed unlimited possibilities, and Mom couldn't tell me what to expect.

On my own again.

"Quinn . . . Quinn. Can you hear me? I need you to listen to me."

His face softened as he continued to stare at me.

"Quinn, it's important. Give me a sign that you understand."

The softness disappeared. Quinn appeared cautious and uncertain. Something triggered his change. Perhaps I was getting through to him.

"Please. Can you hear me? You and Eden and my family are in danger."

Quinn turned away from me. He looked at the young woman again with adoring eyes. "When we are married and we make our home at the hotel, you'll see how special the place will be even if it's not as grand as your parents' home."

Married. The pain ripped through my body.

"I think the hotel is far more grand than this home. Although it has been short-lived, it does have a place in my heart. And my parents won't be so far away. I would be honored to stay at The Maxwell Inn as your wife and to see how the daily operation is conducted," she said confidently.

"Good, because the work ahead of me is fairly substantial, and I would want my future bride to be a part of that life," Quinn said with assurance. He continued to look at her, not glancing up at me this time.

"But there's something that bothers you, beyond the care of your family's work?"

Quinn looked surprised. "How can you read beyond what's said? I assure you, it's just my imagination."

"Something did catch your thoughts, otherwise the abrupt change, or more like a curiosity, took your thoughts away," Eden said.

Quinn chuckled. "Let's not take a strange feeling and turn the moment into something forlorn."

I walked closer to them in order to see both their faces.

"Because, Quinn, my love, we are always aware. That's what makes us different. I, too, have had bouts of uncertainty, which I cannot explain. Yet nothing happens," she said. "I have asked Mother and Father, and I have sought the advice of Dr. Sendal. They have not given me a definitive answer, just the innuendo of possible forces that could work against us. It's the energy around us that keeps life and events in motion. It's so alive. Sometimes I think it makes reading any signs a bit confusing." Eden exhaled, her gaze filled with worry. "I'm feeling a negative force."

Quinn thought for a moment. "I don't feel the turbulence, only the strong energy. And in your family, it's quite strong." His face lit up again. "We have had peace for some time. Perhaps it's the vigilance that makes us too aware." He reached for her, drawing her once more into his arms. "From now on, we keep those visions at bay and focus on the future."

Eden smiled. "To the new century!"

"To our new life." Quinn pulled her close to him and kissed her longingly on the lips. They turned away from the yard, arms linked, and began to walk back to the inviting house.

"Eden, I have to talk to you!" I called out in a strained voice as I reached for the person I wanted to save. *"Get him out of here. Stop him before it's too late!"*

She turned to face me. Her eyes grew weary and the green color of her irises turned paler. Shadows marked her youthful face.

"It's Raefield! He can't be trusted. You must listen to me! Something terrible is going to happen to you and our family!"

Eden reached out for me. I felt hopeful that she could finally hear me.

"Eden, love. What is it?" Quinn asked.

She opened her mouth to say something to him, something even I could hear. Then, she pulled away. Tears began to spill from her eyes.

"Darling, what has gotten you so upset?" Quinn reached for a handkerchief and wiped her face.

Eden looked at Quinn. "Whatever happens, know that my love is always with you."

"Stop this. It's the energy and all the preparations, all of the changes we'll be facing in the new century that's gotten you upset. Come inside now and set aside this gloom." Quinn held her close in his arms.

She looked at me again. This time her face emerged lifeless.

"Eden, don't go." I reached out to her again.

She turned away from me. Quinn led her in the direction of the house. They walked steadily through the garden and disappeared into the fading landscape.

"What am I supposed to do?" I mumbled to myself, exhausted from the knowledge of what I couldn't say. I found a stone bench and sat down to rest. My energy level felt depleted. The spell began to take its toll on me.

Determination surfaced again. *Think, Lauren! Get yourself out of here before you never leave.*

Since I couldn't change the current course of events, at least I could try to warn them. Give them a sign.

I raced back to the house and found my way easily to the room that would hold some answers. This time, I stood outside on the wrap around porch in between the front door and the window of the library. I made sure not to stand in front of him.

". . . It's in the reports. I've had my people keep a running log of the events around New Haven and the major cities in Connecticut. I've also reached out to the other orders and have come up with an unusual trend."

"What are you telling me, Phillip? These acts of violence have been staged?"

"There seems to be a pattern. Look here," my father pointed out. "It's been fairly quiet in certain regions, then pockets of disruption occur in the city near by. It involves common families and wizard families. See here . . . it's the same pattern." My father showed him towns and cities on a map where the incidents occurred. "I've had word from Bridgeport to Providence to Yonkers, New York, and as far as Boston. These occurrences keep appearing in random order, but they're small enough to not draw attention." He looked up at a concerned Raefield. "I think we have a very powerful wizard on our hands."

"It's him, Dad. It's Raefield. He's behind everything!"

"This is most disturbing! I heard rumors of minor incidences, but I didn't make any connection to the type of attack and the people involved. I thought they were random occurrences. And witch families involved! What can we do?" Raefield asked.

My father went silent. He paced the floor of his study. "We must not allow widespread panic. We're still examining the situation and gathering more information. We don't know when the strikes happen and why. The homes have either been burned down, disheveled, or the persons involved have mysteriously disappeared. Very few clues were left behind. We're still trying to understand if the people involved have certain commonalities. The only connection we found linked some of the families involved as acquaintances."

"I see. It's unfortunate that anyone has been involved in this massacre, from *both* sides," Raefield said, putting his hand to his heart. I wanted to aid him in that step by taking it further with a sharp object.

"I appreciate your compassion, Raef. It's refreshing to know we have your support. With people like Stewart and his men trying to undue what has been accomplished, we appreciate those in favor of a more harmonious way of living."

"Of course, of course," Raefield responded sincerely. "I'm in agreement. We need to keep the peace between the two worlds. I *do* believe we can coexist." Raefield moved closer to my father. "What do you make of Stewart?"

"He likes to throw his weight around, but I don't believe he's that clever. Perhaps a distraction," my father began. "No, I would say he might be under the influence of another person—a patronage. I just need more time to look into this."

"Oh, I see."

"If this is all tied. . . ."

"Do tell me what's on your mind," Raefield encouraged.

"I don't wish to trouble you. I'm going to keep these theories to myself for now."

"Oh, no, Phillip. It's no trouble at all."

My father looked appreciatively at Raefield. "I'm so glad we were able to mend the rift between the families. You've been such an important part of our family."

"It's all in the past. We must think of today and hope for a better future."

"Yes . . . yes." My father grasped Raefield's hand as if they had just signed a lasting peace accord. "Now, tell me, Raef. What news has come your way?"

I didn't have to stand closer to the window to hear. I knew the lies coming out of Raefield's mouth would be venomous. Still, it would help to connect the events leading to the present day. Raefield moved closer to my father.

"Phillip, my news is insignificant compared to yours. I'm certain there is no correlation with your theories." Raefield paused, taking in a deep breath. "If you insist, I shall share them with you."

"Please. Anything would be useful."

"It came to me from my own scouts—trusted souls they are. They surveyed the city, and they traveled to Bridgeport and Hartford. They were able to quietly maneuver within groups of people, wizards and commoners alike."

"Yes?"

Raefield sighed again. "Phillip, the only thing I could find were the few examples of burglary that could be connected to Stewart and his people. There had been no bodies found at several of the homes. I was told that certain people may have been so frightened, they left town," he said. "Unfortunately, one of the wizard families, rest their souls, met with an unfortunate evil. I do not know who is responsible."

"I'm already having the police chief look into the matter. Stewart shall be investigated. What about the other cities?"

"A dead end. My men have found no correlation. Only random events of violence that the cities' law enforcement are looking into. We may find reason at a later time."

My father turned thoughtful. "I shall share this news with the other members. We'll still keep watch, but perhaps not be too hasty to act upon these events. Very good, Raefield, for your information."

No, father. Trust your instincts.

"I am with you, and I will be standing beside you."

"Come, let us talk no more of tragic events. Will you join us this evening?" my father asked.

"Thank you, Phillip, but I have a prior engagement. I wish you and your lovely wife a pleasant evening. I shall join you on another occasion."

My father patted Raefield on the back before the two men walked out of the library. Good and loyal friends they had been. I could still warn them. My thoughts scrambled to give them signs of the troubles ahead. They needed a fighting chance! Also, I wanted to say goodbye to my family. Standing here on the inviting porch with my parents so close brought a rush of images to my mind about how my life had been, as well as my days spent with my parents and with Quinn. My father had been the mayor. He had important work ahead of him. I was to be married. I would live at the Maxwell Inn. I had known Quinn's family. The turn of the century neared. . . .

As I imagined the days of old New Haven, the sky dramatically darkened in a stormy gray layer. The wind howled against the mighty Victorian. I looked up. I no longer stood on the front porch. The air turned icy. The windows and the shutters collided against each other, and the great oak tree in the front lawn swayed back and forth. I remembered Mom telling me about the majestic oak tree that stood in front of the house before being replaced by the sugar maple. I looked down at my arms. I suddenly faded.

"No, not yet! There's so much more I need to do."

The stained glass front door blew open for the uninvited wind to come through.

"Heavens, are we in for a storm?" a man's voice called out. It could only be Nathan's. I swear I've heard this voice before.

"Perhaps Mother Nature is teasing us today with what is to come. Close the door, good man, or you'll catch an early death," my father called out to him.

Nathan stood behind the artful door with the shadows on his back. I still couldn't see him.

"Father . . . please. I'm here. Don't turn away from me."

I ran toward the house. My face and hands touched the glass partition. I pushed and kicked and reached for the door handle, but I couldn't get through.

"I'm not ready. I have to tell you so much. I have to warn you!" I called out for the last time, trying to convince myself that I could make a difference. Something moved me away from the door. I watched as my body faded even more into the air.

"Mom, hear me! I'm not ready. I need more time."

My calls remained unheard. The same porch I'd stood upon faded away. My Victorian home moved farther and farther away from me. It appeared helpless and deserted; its timeless colors grew somber under the ashen and angry sky.

The wind gained speed, relentless in its seeming determination to blow the house down. I lacked powers in this domain. I dwindled into a fine mist. Yet, moments before my departure, I looked up for the last time at my once beautiful home to see a man—he stood at the window of my parents' room. He looked regal and convincing. He stood there for everyone to see—no fear in his eyes, only a satisfied grin to match his victorious facial expression. No one knew he watched. Then, the flames sprang forth from nowhere. They climbed. They consumed the magnificent Queen Anne. I recalled the fire that had raged in my home and changed my existence. I closed my eyes to banish the image of my lost home and to escape the wicked laugh that followed. I couldn't save them, and I couldn't save me.

6

FACES AND PLACES

The images moved so fast, flashed on a screen in rapid succession. With my eyes still closed, I heard Mom chanting in a foreign tongue. I opened my eyes to the tight formation we'd devised. Mom spoke the last few phrases before finishing her wondrous spell. All eyes gazed upon me again with hesitation and fear, as well as a mix of curiosity. I let go of those bonds.

"Lauren?"

I turned away from Mom. I didn't want to see her eyes, searching for answers. I walked over to the grand window—the very same window that my mother had looked out of—and I stared out toward the east on a warmer day. The afternoon sun felt surprisingly warm on my face.

"I'm going to the car and get something to drink. I'm sure we could all use it," Isaak suggested. "I don't know about you, but all this hocus pocus has really wiped me out."

"I think I'll join you. I could use a little fresh air," Chelsea added. They quickly left the tense room. I heard the door swiftly close behind them.

I continued to stare out of the tall windows to review everything that had just happened. I don't know what I hoped to gain from standing here. It's not like I could see them again.

"You don't have to say anything," I told Quinn, who now stood behind me.

"I just wanted to say that I'm glad you're back," he said in a low voice.

I turned to face his steady gaze. It seemed like forever since I'd last seen his eyes. "Really, I'm actually doing better than I expected. A little tired, maybe, but not out."

"It's just . . . it must've been a shock for you to be there."

My head spun. I knew they were waiting for answers. "It was definitely eye-opening, but I'm glad I went. It was more than I expected. I really could've used more time," I finally confessed. "Was I gone for long?"

Before Quinn could answer, Mom eased closer to me. "For you, it probably felt like hours. Time moved quickly. For us, it was more like thirty minutes. The energy to pull it off was overwhelming. She turned to look at Isaak and Chelsea, who'd returned from their great escape. They gave her what she wanted.

"Take this. It'll do you some good," Mom said, handing over the chilled, homemade brew.

I lifted up the drink in a toast. "To a rapid salvation."

"I'll drink to that," Isaak chimed in as he quickly finished his concoction. "There. I'll be good as new in no time."

I could now look at her. "Mom, she was beautiful. And my father couldn't have been a better person. I can see them now permanently etched in my mind." I thought of the guileful man, as well.

Everyone moved closer to me. We found ourselves sitting on the forbidden, "for display only" furniture. Today marked an exceptional day, so I don't think it would matter.

She held back her tears. "They *are* wonderful people. Don't ever doubt that. I wish you could've had more time with them, but with anything that has to do with time, it's simply unpredictable. Whether it's traveling through time or sending you back for even a glimpse, it's uncontrollable. I don't know if I can do that again."

Dad finally spoke up. "Where did you actually end up?"

"Here, right in this very same room. I guess it was a year or two before 1900. Some major events were going to take place."

Quinn's eyes softened. He waited patiently as I continued.

"There seems to be gaps. I wasn't able to find out everything." His eyes retreated, yet remained understanding. I looked at him warmly. "Eden was a lovely name."

"Lauren is just as good."

My parents stepped away from us. They walked over to talk to Chelsea and Isaak.

"What took you so long to find me?"

Quinn stared back at me with his brilliant eyes and the warmest of smiles. "It was just a matter of time."

"Time, that's all we needed."

My family moved in closer again. "We hadn't lived here for very long, but I guess in reality, we never made it that long before everything changed. Besides seeing my parents, I saw my former governess, Clara, and I heard Nathan speak to my family. I didn't see his face. They seemed like important members of the family."

"Yes, they were loyal to your parents," Mom added.

"My father was working on leads he'd received about some events that were happening around town and in the other cities across the East coast. He said they were small enough to not draw attention."

"Yes, I remember your father telling us this not too long after he'd gotten the news. At the time, we couldn't make any connections, just random witches and regular people had vanished or perished. Only later did we realize who was behind all of it," Dad said. "But we knew it had to be another witch to take out one of us."

"It sounded like a man named Stuart was the scapegoat, although I'm not sure how involved he was."

"He had some direct involvement, but he couldn't be tied to any deaths," Dad continued, his facial expression skeptical. "In the end, however, Stewart was found guilty. They publicly executed him along with a few of his men. I assumed he was already dying. The public display just made it more convincing."

I felt somber about the inhumanity one could inflict on others. "My father confided in Raefield." I finally said his name aloud. I looked up at Mom. "You're right. He does have a way with people. There's something about him that's horribly appealing."

Mom closed her eyes as she nodded. "He does that to people. He draws them in. It's his energy that attracts people or the way he talks to them. Or it's his angelic face that everyone sees. I don't know. I'm . . . ashamed to have fallen for it." She lowered her face.

I reached for her hand. "You didn't know. I fell for it, too, obviously. Even when I stood before him, I was drawn to him. My parents trusted him."

"We all did," Quinn added. "He was very powerful."

"He was," I said, thinking back to the ugly side of Raefield that I saw and how he'd stood there at the window.

How much did he know? That thought played over and over in my mind. I forced the idea away. It's over with; it no longer mattered. The events were part of history.

I looked up at Dad. "My father mentioned having theories about these missing people and the fatal incidents, which he didn't want to share with Raefield at the time. Could he have suspected Raefield?"

Mom and Dad glanced at each other. "He didn't mention anything to us. Your mother didn't say anything, either. Even to the bitter end, they never denounced Raefield. If he suspected anything was connected to Raefield, your father kept it to himself," Mom blurted out.

"Why, Phillip? What didn't you tell us?"

Dad reached for her. "Helen, if he knew, he probably had good reasons to keep it to himself. Even though Phillip was wise and powerful, Raefield was extremely cunning. If he exposed Raefield too soon, or if Raefield suspected that they knew he was behind all of this treachery, Raefield could've retaliated much sooner. They welcomed him into their lives. He always visited their home. I'm not sure what he would've done to the family," Dad reminded us. "In hindsight, Raefield always seemed two steps ahead."

"I wouldn't have welcomed him. And I know my parents wouldn't have either, if it hadn't been for the information they sought."

Mom looked at me thoughtfully, then she turned to Dad. "Perhaps you're right. If Phillip knew, he would've needed concrete evidence to show the other members. I don't know if they would've been able to stop Raefield. I'm not even sure if some of the other members weren't corrupt. Raefield's control was far reaching."

I believed my parents did their best, despite having the enemy right in their home. It was time to leave this broken place, I decided.

Isaak stepped forward. "I think I've had enough art relics and history for one day. We should get out of here before these walls suck us in."

Chelsea leaned closer to him. "Well, for once big brother, I'm in total agreement. I'm ready to move on."

"Mom, if you don't mind, I'd like to take one last look upstairs. I don't think I'll be back here for some time."

"Are you sure about this?"

"I'll go with you," Quinn suggested.

"It's my house. I need to do this alone. I want to say goodbye," I said.

Quinn looked at me skeptically. "Just holler if you notice anything. Don't be too long, because I'll come up there if you're not down here soon."

"Got it."

Isaak was on my heels. "Why don't we escort you to the stairs before we head out the door? It's the least we can do."

"Suit yourself."

"We'll be waiting for you here," Mom muttered.

The three of us walked under the grand arch and into the long hallway for a final time. I had no plans to return here unless it would be truly helpful. Would this be my only gateway into my former life so that I could learn what conspired within the last year of that past existence? There should have been another portal into that life.

"Are you sure you want to do this?" Chelsea asked me as we stood at the bottom of the impressive stairway. It appeared much longer than I remembered.

I nodded. "I have to. As much as I love this place, as much as it seems to hold remarkable powers, it seems to want me here too much. Like it doesn't want to let me go."

"I'll say," Isaak remarked. "I tell you, this house is very

much alive. And if we don't leave here soon, I think this place will lock us in with you, Lauren, being its first prey."

"No, I don't think this place wants to physically harm any of us. I think it's trying to tell me something."

"Like I said. It gives me the creeps. Let's go, Chelsea, so that Lauren can have her farewell. We'll be outside in the real world if you need us." Isaak grabbed Chelsea's hand and led her out through the stained-glass door and onto the covered porch until they walked past the gated yard into the safe, open world situated beyond my Victorian dream.

I turned to the faded floral carpet that clung tightly to the wooden staircase, still fresh in my mind, as I had seen it when it was brand new. My body shifted ahead to the darkened platform waiting for me at the top of the stairs. I took that first step. The floorboard creaked with every other step I took, but was silenced by my racing heart as I came closer and closer to the room that drew me in. I was ready.

The hallway looked less familiar. Instead of an inviting and illuminating passage, only somberness hovered around me. All the doors were closed, and it seemed as though the sun had deliberately forgotten the second floor. I looked directly at the room that had once been mine. A crack remained open for particles of light to escape.

"Lauren."

I walked toward the room, cautious and excited once again. The door opened as I neared, the sun blinding me when I reached the gate of her domain. *My haven.*

I walked into its warmth and its embrace, and I felt the exuberance filling my room. The energy felt electrifying. Everything stirred inside of me. It had waited for me, hoping that I would return. And I had. The bedroom was truly awake and alive.

"I'm here. Tell me what I need to know."

Silence permeated. Energy remained and stirred around me and inside of me. I walked around the airy room and studied the bedroom with my patience intact. I could wait as long as it took to find the answers.

"I'll leave, and I'll never come back. Is that what you want?"

Again, I was met with silence. The voice no longer felt close to me. I extended my hands. I wasn't sure if it decided to leave me all together. I stood there for a few moments before lowering my hands. Then the air around me began to swirl. First, it moved in a slow fashion before picking up speed. Next, the curtains began to sway from the wind whipping through the air. This new force muted the hum of the central air. I turned my head abruptly to the window as it was suddenly forced open. I quickly went to the scene.

I stood at the window for some time as I might have in the Victorian days. Had I often looked outside and beyond the invisible lines of my home? Had I seen what I now couldn't physically see?

"Lauren, it's dangerous."

I knew she hadn't truly left me. She wanted me here. I looked outside again, far beyond the horizon. It became clear. I saw what felt incredibly important and what was forbidden.

"I know what I have to do."

"Please, Lauren. Stay."

I ignored her warning. I felt in control. I would persevere.

The pounding on the door shattered my hypnotic state.

"Lauren, open the door! What's going on inside?" Quinn shouted. He pounded on the door and shook the doorknob. *"Open this damn door!"*

I calmly crossed the room and opened the door. Quinn nearly fell into the room.

"What's wrong?"

"What do you mean, 'What's wrong?'" Quinn yelled, but not as loudly as before. "We've waited for you downstairs, and we've called you but you didn't answer. I've been pounding on this door, and you didn't respond. Why is the door locked?"

"It wasn't. I was just walking around. I wanted to spend some more time in here, as I said earlier."

Quinn released a heavy sigh. "You were gone too long. We thought something had happened to you. What went on in here?"

"Nothing. I'm perfectly fine. Nothing will happen to me here. I only wanted to remember."

"Lauren, it doesn't happen that way," Quinn said in a gentler voice. He no longer sounded annoyed. He appeared to understand.

"We can go now. I have what I need." I turned and surveyed the calm room. The window was closed again, and the air was still. The humming air conditioner resumed its course. I took Quinn's hand, leading him out of my room.

"Lauren . . ." said the voice, echoing in the air. And just as the door had flown wide open, I closed off the room to my past.

We hurried down the staircase to my waiting parents. Their frowns nearly matched the one Quinn had worn moments earlier.

"Lauren, I'm not going to ask you again," Mom began. "No, I'm going to insist and demand this from you. Whatever you think you're doing, or whatever you think you can handle alone, *please,* let us help you. We're on your side.

These are powers that we don't fully understand. We have forces coming from different directions, and we don't know if they're always friendly. So, please, *don't* shut us out."

"I know. I'm sorry I've been so closed off. I just needed some time to think and to clear my head. The past is rather haunting. It's helped me to be here so that I can try to let go of that life."

Mom nodded. She put her arm around my shoulder. "I know it's been difficult for you, sweetie. I just want you to know you're not alone. We're going to see this through. Together."

"Okay."

"Let's go back to the hotel."

The four of us left by the stained glass door, my past in our wake and my present trapped in the room upstairs. I turned my head to see the curtains flying around my parents' former room, and I knew it was far from being over. I closed my eyes to shut off the other side, but I felt its strength.

"Lauren, don't go."

*

We devoured a feast even though we had tasted the potent drink that should have kept us strong. We didn't want to take any chances just in case we needed to use ample amount of magic. New Haven seemed to contain many surprises this time around.

"I think we should call it an early night and preserve what energy we have left. Let's get an early start for Bridgeport, spend a day or two there and along the coast, then head north for Hartford and then return to New Haven before we fly out. The rest of the time should be a non-working vacation," Mom announced at the dinner table. She looked at Isaak.

"What?"

"Now's your chance to decide what kind of fun we'll have," Chelsea suggested.

"Leave it to me to make this happen." Isaak rubbed his palms together as though about to perform the greatest magic trick ever.

*

Just after nine, my family went to their rooms in order to go to bed. I still needed to pack for tomorrow. I looked forward to leaving New Haven for the next city. Since the beginning of this trip, I'd often felt as if I'd never left New Haven, and I also experienced uneasiness at just being in this city. Not a good idea to come here? I never regretted seeing my birth parents. Joy and a sense of ease had overwhelmed me, knowing they had lived a good life.

"I don't know about you, but I'm exhausted. I can't seem to keep my eyes open," Quinn said between yawns.

"I'm really not that tired. The energy boost is keeping me awake. I think I'll watch TV in bed. That might help."

"Suit yourself. Just lie next to me so that I know you're close by."

I climbed into bed, aware it wouldn't be long before Quinn would fall into a deep sleep. He put his arms around me. He felt warm and real, not like a ghost or a spirit haunting me.

"Are you going to tell me what happened in your room today?" Quinn asked, his eyes barely open. "Your mom told me she found you talking to yourself before we did the spell. We both know that isn't true." Quinn yawned. "And before we left the house, you had another encounter. What did you learn behind those locked doors?"

"I'm not completely sure yet. I don't know what to make of it."

Quinn's eyes closed. "When you're ready to . . . tell me . . . what you know . . . I'll listen. . . ."

He fell fast asleep. Soon, he'd be in the deepest of sleep, unable to wake up easily. On another occasion, we'd talk about this misunderstanding. We would also talk about some of the things he'd forgotten to mention. He'd tell me his version of what I was like back in old New Haven when he knew me. He'd tell me about how we met and lived and if we ever married. None of this would happen tonight. After this night ended, I wasn't even certain he'd still want to marry me.

"Forgive me, Quinn," I whispered

I grabbed my purse and the keys to the Civic, and I quietly slipped out the door and into the dimly lighted hallway of the hotel. I heard a few voices and televisions blaring behind closed doors. I carefully walked passed the mystical room, which had called on me in my unconscious state, fearing that I would be drawn into its clutches again. I ignored the blue and white light that suddenly shone from beneath the door of the forbidden room.

"Come to me, Lauren."

I refused to look back. My exit to the elevator and down into the lobby came swiftly. The hotel clerk had his back to me as I sped unnoticed through the door and out into the haunting night. Just as I reached my getaway car, the distant-sounding moans that I had heard in Chicago called out to me again. A low and quiet pitch—an agonizing tone. It wavered and rattled against the air. I shut out the distracting noise to stay focused on my agenda as I sped off in my car down an unknown road.

Did I have a plan? No, only strength of will and sheer determination to see this night through and to end all disturbances. I prepared myself for a long and arduous night. It would come down to me. It would end with me as the final act.

The streets were dimly lit, quiet and balmy from the humid night. My car hummed along the narrow road, and I made quick turns in order to reach my destination. I had mapped out his place from the beginning, even before I'd been summoned to it.

As I neared his place, the road turned off into an isolated location. It became narrow and distant from the rest of the city. The trees appeared much thicker, the moon hidden away in the distant sky. It appeared to be afraid to show its face. I saw only a few homes bordering the estate to protect itself from outsiders. Even in the dead of night, creatures roamed the wooded terrain.

I turned into the curved driveway in front of the grand estate. The iron gate had, surprisingly, been left open. I mentally prepared myself for what lay ahead.

From what I could see in the dark, the mansion appeared well-kept, even formidable. The deep red brick, Renaissance-style home stood grandly and spanned a full city block. The Historical Society had neatly placed outdoor lighting along the rim of the yard to illuminate the home. A single lamppost along the walkway to the main door, which appeared to have been constructed at the time the mansion had been built, flickered on and off when I passed by. I looked up at the sky again to see the moon still hidden from the earth. No signs guided me tonight. Once I entered his place, I might never escape. I reached for the door with a trembling hand.

"Stay with me, Lauren."

I quickly turned around and searched for the location of the familiar voice, aware that I was still alone. I stood at the enemy's door with the spirits of yesteryear shadowing my every step. Taking in a deep breath, I pushed open the unlocked double doors and stepped inside.

The foyer reached as high as the one in my parents' home, but on a much larger and more formal scale. I stood in awe of the great open space before me. The towering windows behind me allowed the night inside, which shimmered against the reflection cast by the granite staircase in front of me. I noticed the balcony on the second floor; the rooms remained concealed by the darkness. Only the reflection from the outside lights bouncing off of the crystal chandelier above gave me comfort.

I turned to my right and discovered an elegant and spacious living room, once known as a formal parlor. The curtains remained opened to admit natural light. My curiosity surpassed this formal room and focused on the two closed doors on the far side of the parlor. I didn't hesitate. I wanted to know more.

Slowly, I turned the knob. The door creaked loudly when I pushed it opened. The curtains that faced the front of the home were closed, allowing only the opaque outlines to be seen. The room smelled musty and felt cold. It resembled a gentlemen's retreat. I grabbed my flashlight from my sack to search for the light switch. I knew Raefield would incorporate the most modern amenities that money could buy. My flashlight revealed high quality wood paneling of rich cherry.

To my surprise, the room proved to be substantially long. I stood in his fully furnished billiards hall. The fireplace on the left wall stood massive and ornately designed, but something else caught my attention aside from the flickering of the modest chandelier that illuminated the room. I walked over to the strange finding. At the base of the fireplace, I saw ashes still deep in color and the shadows of smoke seeping into the air.

A power surge resonated in me.

I quickly left the room as I found it and ran to the grand foyer. My heart raced. I scanned the upstairs balcony, the area to my left, and then the large rooms that loomed ahead.

"You can't turn back now, Lauren," I whispered out loud.

This needed to end. Tonight.

Then, I noticed a shimmering light coming from behind the other door of the parlor. Another distinctive room, I assumed. Grabbing my special bracelet, I hid myself from the world like the spirits of the night.

I moved through the foyer and into the parlor like air, leaving no footsteps behind. No furniture would be touched, no door opened. I arrived at the towering, wooden door painted in a soft hue. What lurked behind this sweet door? My instincts urged me forward in my quest.

Drawing in another deep breath, I approached the door and easily moved through it. I stood in Raefield's library, his personal office. This room put my father's office and his Victorian library to shame. Raefield's library was elaborate and masculine. Formal furniture filled the space and another fireplace occupied the same wall opposite the one in the billiards room. I stared at the sizable, mahogany desk, which must've been where Raefield conducted business in his arrogant and cunning ways. I wanted to take an ax and chop the table in half.

The lights continued to flicker in a growing succession.

"It's dangerous here. Leave before the change."

The voice startled me. I knew her voice, the voice of my Victorian past. I looked at the emptiness around me. I was invisible, yet she still followed me.

"*Hurry!*"

I made a dash for the door, but I froze in what began to form within Raefield's private room. The light turned mesmerizing. It swirled. It grew larger. The brightness dimmed, then became overshadowed by a pale blue mist coming from nowhere.

"*Nooo!*"

I couldn't move more than a few inches. It held me in its grip in this room. The lights on the walls and the ceiling lights grew brighter again as the mist moved in front of my eyes. I continued to push with all of my strength, my sole desire to leave this forsaken room. Clenching my fists, I forced the energy inside of me free.

The mist turned denser as the blue hue deepened in color. Horror unfolded before my eyes. I knew I needed to leave. The energy continued to circumvent inside and around me to free me of my bondage. Everything came alive. The invisible grip on me loosened, yet I still remained its hostage.

I faded in and out of invisibility. I would run out of time before the room completely changed. My mind quickly focused on the energy I cultivated. I let go of all the strength I possessed.

Every object not weighted down in the room floated in the air. Hand crafted pillows, ornamental figurines, and all the items on Raefield's desk danced free of gravity. Volumes removed themselves from the bookshelves. They moved in random motion, filling the air like birds. Even my hair floated in several different directions.

The room lit up like stadium lights. The color schemata

became intangible as my energy competed with the power of the mist. I saw it grow and gain strength as my powers turned willful. I intended to win. Then, the mist began to break away. An empty hole formed at the center of this mysterious and threatening vapor, but its powers never relented. I remained trapped.

I shook, but I persevered until the library trembled. I would bring this house down if needed in order to free myself. I wouldn't die here, trapped like a caged animal. Just as I felt freedom reigning in closer, the hole began to fill. The center of the mist shaped into an obscure form. It swirled and it thickened with cloud-like vapors for a few moments before the gases dispersed. Shadows and light took over the misty center. An outline began to take shape. My heart raced within my pressure-filled chest.

By this time, I was nearly free. Just a little bit longer and I would run from this place like the stupid person who should've known better. But I wasn't fast enough. The form grew. A profile turned clearer and appeared real in front of me. I knew those eyes. *His* eyes, his gripping and wicked eyes stared back at me. I concentrated fully in order to free myself. My last chance. The erratic energy forced the loose objects to move in increasing disarray around the library.

A malicious grin formed on Raefield's lips. I'd heard the same condescending laughter in the back of my mind. It had resonated from my parents' Queen Anne home. He would call this victory. He would complete what he had set out to do. That alone gave me the determination to finish what I planned to do.

Fight him tonight.

Raefield's presence floated in limbo. He wasn't completely formed. His perfect skin, his albino blond hair, and his bright green eyes reflected a projection. I had moments to spare. . . .

"You can't take me."

Raefield extended his arm through the great mist. He reached for my neck. I inched away from his wrathful grip. Raefield laughed. The laughter was silent. He laughed and he laughed until his spiteful eyes turned red. Raefield continued to laugh, this time his voice sounded. I felt his victory as he overcame. He called upon the mist. His demising calls irritated my ears. It hovered and it grew until his maddening voice echoed throughout the library. He then reached full form.

"Nooo!"

Surprised at what I'd just done, the room shook uncontrollably. My energy reached octave levels. The mist began to pull back, weakening at points. It no longer appeared vivid. I saw the shock in Raefield's eyes. He started to fade. The look on his face remained spiteful. He scrambled to keep his present form intact. The mist closing became my salvation. Its purpose had not been completed. I remained confused by Raefield's true motive. Sending Raefield back to his world remained my only goal at this moment.

As the surge continued, I won my freedom. I ran out of the room, through the parlor and out to the front door I'd once foolishly entered. I reached for the door handle to make my great escape. The door refused to open. I pushed and I pulled to no avail. I pounded on the door and pulled at it again. Still, the door wouldn't open. I forced the energy out of me to do my will. Nothing happened.

"Ha ha ha ha ha!" cried the echoes of Raefield's laughter.

Thinking back to the trick that Dr. Sendal had taught me

about rapid movement, I spun my way to freedom. In no time, I moved like molecules to the other side. When I stopped moving, I still faced the front door from the inside. I grabbed my bag and raced for the other rooms, knowing every home had a back door. The grand room appeared ominous in the dark. The double glass doors to the veranda remained uncovered, allowing the night sky to cascade into the central room of the home. I immediately grabbed the handles.

"Why? Why can't you open up for me?"

I didn't waste time arguing with a door. I ran out of the grand room and glanced back at the library through the parlor's door to see if the mist disappeared. Light hues floated in the air, but I didn't see Raefield. If he'd come through, he would've found me by now. The kitchen entrance through the darkened hallway led into the servants' quarters. It resembled my parents' home, only twice as large. The small back door hid in the background. It was my last hope to escape.

"C'mon. Open up for me." I banged on the door. I jerked at the doorknob. My powers focused on opening the door. It didn't work. I was stuck. I was trapped in here until whatever force controlled this house finally let go.

"There has to be a way out," I whispered.

I wouldn't give up. Anxiety crept inside of me when my thoughts turned to the possibility of never leaving this place. I shut down the disturbing thought. A pounding at the front door startled me. I came to a standstill. Did Raefield pass through? My defenses went up again.

"Lauren? Where are you?" Chelsea called out from the foyer.

"I'm here!" I ran out of the kitchen to the foyer where

she and my father stood, looking confused and relieved.

"Are you hurt?" Dad asked.

"No, I'm fine. I've been stuck here. How did you know? How did you get in?"

Dad looked at Chelsea then back at me. "Quinn called Isaak. He was very drowsy. We put it together that you might be here. Lauren, *what* were you thinking?"

"I'm . . . sorry. I thought that I could take care of this." I lowered my head in shame. "Is Quinn here?"

"He's still back at the hotel . . . recuperating," Chelsea responded.

"We'll talk later. Let's get out of here. I don't know how long your mother can hold this. Quinn and I would've been the best people to get you out of here, but the three of us managed to unlock the door."

I looked at Dad strangely. I wasn't sure what he meant regarding the best people. Chelsea, Dad, and I easily fled from Raefield's mansion into the open where Mom stood with her palms out, chanting in that ancient language of hers, which she used to send me back in time.

"Paz de' tŭe! Paz de' tŭe! Sèla bä'hlan mé pâllenräe ÿ chŏyan bë' penèz ăblet'ÿ ăjelŏp îo meap naelå. Ăblet'ÿ phtémyt. Blâve paz! Blâve rhÿ!"

Mom stopped chanting when we approached her. There was no time for words. We all looked at the sky above Raefield's estate. A pale blue and fading mist left his home, then dispersed into the sky until it vanished.

Mom looked at me with bloodshot eyes. "First thing tomorrow morning, we're leaving."

7

CONFESSIONS

The drive to the airport was uncomfortably silent just like
the first few moments after takeoff. I reached for Quinn's
hand only to have him pull it away.

"I'm sorry, Quinn. I would never harm you. You know
that. It was stupid of me to go there. I thought I was doing
the right thing."

"I wasn't harmed. And yes, it was reckless of you to go
there."

"I know that now. I want you to understand that what I
did was completely irresponsible and stupid. I've learned my
lesson," I said as I pleaded my case. "Quinn, will you ever
forgive me?"

He stared at me for a few moments, his gray eyes dull and
uninviting. "I'm tired. I need to get my strength back."
Quinn turned his back to me.

I stared out into the aisle and out of the window next to
Quinn. I felt tired, but I couldn't sleep. Last night seemed to
go on forever after my family found me at Raefield's place.
My father managed to say goodnight to me once we reached
the hotel; my mother didn't say two words. The final blow
to my ego was delivered when Quinn switched rooms with

Chelsea. My sister looked sympathetic, advising, "Give it time."

I pictured those angry green eyes staring back at me before they disappeared into the mist, and I flashbacked to my parents' home when I'd watched the interaction between Raefield and my parents. I erased those disturbing thoughts from my mind.

After some time, I finally managed to drift into a hazy sleep. Not long after my last conscious thought, the plane landing startled me awake.

"Ladies and Gentlemen, we'll taxi to the gate in a few minutes. Please remain in your seat with your seatbelt fastened until we have turned off the seatbelt sign. Welcome to Chicago."

Home. We'd finally made it home, far away from the awful clutches of what could've been an actual and disastrous event known as Raefield. Still, I'd managed to finally see my parents and how they lived. That became my only consolation after disappointing my current family and Quinn.

The early flight out of Connecticut and the time change left me drained. It didn't matter, anyway. We didn't say more than a few polite words, just like strangers. And our plans to leave my family could now be eliminated, which alleviated some of the guilt I carried. I only wanted to sleep for a long time.

Isaak patted me on the back. "Don't be so hard on yourself."

Standing at the luggage carousel, Mom managed to talk about what she'd make for dinner tonight and asked me when I'd be over.

Quinn mumbled, "I'm getting the luggage. It's rush hour."

I followed quietly behind him into the parking structure. Once inside the car and after we headed down the freeway, my eyes closed off to the outside world. I felt afraid to even look at him. I didn't want to push my luck. Time needed to be on my side. However, the little knot in my stomach told me otherwise.

*

"What are you doing back so soon? I thought you had at least three more days in Connecticut," a startled Raegan asked, looking up from the couch when I walked through the front door. The TV blared in the background with some morning talk show. She still wore her pajamas while playing with Oscar.

"Plans changed. It's too long of a story to get into."

"Uh, oh. Tell me about it." Raegan turned down the volume.

"It'll have to wait. I'm exhausted. I didn't get much sleep since we left so early," I said, dragging my luggage to the stairs. I couldn't stop yawning.

"Darn. And we were going to have a block party while you were gone."

"You'd have one without me?"

"No. I wanted to see what you'd say. It's still an idea we could have," Raegan said. Her warm grin slightly lifted my mood.

"That would be something."

Raegan faced the front door. "Did I hear the other door open? Where's Quinn?"

"He had a long night. He wanted to get some rest."

"Right. What happened?"

"Is it that obvious?"

"No. I just know you well." Raegan turned off the TV, her eyes focused on me.

I took in a deep breath. "I'll tell you later. I'm too exhausted to go over the details again. We're . . . having a misunderstanding. It was a pretty quiet ride home."

"Oh, I see."

"Yeah."

"Well, you can't stop there. What happened?" Raegan asked.

I shook my head. "I did some really dumb things, because I thought it was the right thing to do, and it ended up blowing up in my face. And my family had to come to my rescue. Quinn is still a little sore with me."

"Geez, Lauren. What did you do to get Quinn so mad at you?"

"C'mon, Raegan. Aren't you on my side?"

"I'm sorry. I didn't mean it that way. Of course, I'm on your side. Whatever you did, I'm sure you meant well. It's just . . . he *cares* about you so much that for him to give you the cold shoulder, he must be pretty upset. Just give him time."

"That's what Chelsea said."

My guilt surfaced again. Raegan only reminded me of how much he cared, I told myself, and that I might have jeopardized that trust. *I'm sorry that I hurt you.*

"You'll love us forever, won't you? No matter what?" Raegan cooed. Oscar made himself quite comfortable on Raegan's lap.

"I'm going to take a nap." I headed up the stairs with my belongings and survival kit that I didn't use. I felt my bed calling. Later on when my head cleared up, I would deal with Quinn.

I didn't unpack my suitcase, only removed the jewelry box from my backpack. At least that stayed quiet during the entire trip—one less puzzle to try to sort out. My fingers found the grooved edges. What other clue should've emerged from the box, which housed my bracelet? It wouldn't tell me on command. It had its own mind that sprang out new messages. Out of sheer curiosity, I opened up my jewelry box. Nothing changed. My fingers went over every side and every corner of the magical box without finding any new clues. Carefully, I lifted the ruby velvet covering as I did before. No note and no signs of forced entry. I closed the box and put it away for safekeeping.

I grabbed my phone and let my fingers move freely.

When can I see you?

It was his move. He probably slept, so after he rested, he'd contact me. I mentally crossed my fingers. Setting my phone aside, I reached inside my purse for a piece of my past. The second message stared me in the face from my misadventure of the previous night.

The Coming Storm

The note really puzzled me after I received it. I remembered running to the room thinking Quinn was in trouble. Then, I thought it referred to the trip to Connecticut, which made sense to think the message had to do with New Haven and events surrounding Raefield. Therefore, I made preparations. I saw the mist in his library, and I witnessed Raefield in the present day. Thinking back now, it was just an illusion of him. Mom thought a spell had been placed on his estate, the kind that tied me to his home like a trap. Of course, I fell for it. So why did I feel this meant something more? Whatever the reasons, the mystery of my past still unfolded.

My eyes barely stayed open. I managed to reach for my phone on the nightstand. Quinn still hadn't called. *Asleep, he's just asleep.* I put away the phone and sank back into my bed. I couldn't fight my exhaustion any longer. Everything I wanted to think about and planned to do suddenly slipped from my mind.

*

Where am I?

I thought I slept into the next day. I felt as if we'd been gone for weeks and had returned home to the pleasant surroundings that I missed whenever I traveled. I knew I needed sleep, but not through an entire day. Work to do!

Just relax, Lauren. It's only a few extra minutes more.

7:15 pm.

Raegan didn't wake me up. What a considerate friend. I grabbed my phone from the stand and checked my messages: two from Mom, one from Chelsea, and one from Elsie. No messages from Quinn. I tried not to sulk.

Raegan probably told everyone of "a sudden change in plans that caused them to come home right away" otherwise Elsie wouldn't have called unless it was important. I could see the gang now, all huddling together and coming up with plans A, B, and C. Plan B had been in motion if not for my foolish and rookie decision, which caused Quinn to give me the silent treatment. I kept plan B on hold, but I reserved the option to move to plan C, whatever that might be. I touched my growling stomach. A whole day had passed since I'd eaten! My reserves would be depleted very soon. I grabbed my robe and headed down the hallway. The TV sounded quite loud.

"Hey, there, sunshine. You're finally up. Did we wake you?" Raegan asked.

"No, I woke up on my own," I mumbled as I descended the stairs. "Alex."

"You're looking stellar," Alex said. Raegan jabbed him in his side. "What?"

"Men," she replied.

"It's okay. I'm sure I'm not looking my best. Besides, I never listen to anything Alex has to say."

"No kidding," Alex replied.

"What did I miss?"

"You mean in the last two days? How about life?" Raegan informed me.

"*What?* I slept that long? Why didn't you wake me up?"

"Obviously, you needed the sleep. Nothing would've shaken you from your slumber. I'm sure a tornado could've blown through, and you'd still be all snuggled in your bed," Alex remarked. He looked at me suspiciously. "What did you take?"

"What's that supposed to mean?"

"You heard me. I'd be depleted by now. Although sleep does slow things down," Alex replied.

"*Alex,*" Raegan warned.

He glanced at her. "I'm not accusing her of anything. I know she's not that kind of person. I'm just curious in regards to her health. She should share her little secret."

"Really, Alex. I didn't take anything. I would've remembered." I moved closer to the large bay window in the living room and plopped myself down on the ledge. "It was an unusual vacation—eventful and productive—definitely worth going." I turned my back to them. I looked out at the sky. The sun would set in another hour. "Two days, huh?" I mumbled. My thoughts turned to Quinn again. I felt Alex's stare on my back, but I didn't care.

"When you're ready to inform the rest of us about your longevity trick, we'll be listening," he said.

"I don't know about you, Lauren, but I'd be starving by now. I ordered food. There's plenty in the fridge," Raegan said.

I quickly turned to her. "Don't mind if I do." I walked into the kitchen for my mini-feast. She had stocked pasta, salad, pizza, breadsticks, fruit slices, dessert, and beverages. I craved something sweet. Actually, I craved everything. I laid out what I wanted.

"Where's Quinn?" Alex asked.

"*Alex,*" Raegan said.

"I was just asking."

"Sorry, Lauren," Raegan said.

"I mean, he's not here and I'm surprised he isn't, that's all," Alex said in an innocent voice.

Raegan rolled her eyes.

"It's fine. Like I said, I tend to ignore him." I took a bite of the food in front of me.

Alex cleared his throat. "That's not very nice, Lauren. Can't I be a little concerned about your boyfriend? After all, every time some event happens—case in point, your barbecue party—the ghosts of Christmas past show up. It seems rather odd."

I stopped eating and gulped down some juice. I turned to face Alex. "This has nothing to do with Quinn. It's all about me. It's something that I did to provoke the past."

"What happened in Connecticut?" Alex probed, genuine concern appearing on his face.

"Let's just say I was trying to take care of nuisances, and it backfired."

"I gathered that much. No wonder Quinn is giving you the silent treatment. I would, too," Alex said.

"Seriously, Alex," Raegan commented.

"I'm not provoking her. I just want to know what she did to cause a rift. It doesn't bother me. He's not my favorite person, but at least I don't think less of him this time."

"Well, I'm sure you're not his favorite person, either," Raegan responded.

"That, I know, is true. I just want to know what went down."

I ignored him. I savored the luscious meal in front of me. It felt so good to eat again. I knew I'd missed something. Sleep felt refreshing, but this completed my existence. A whole Lauren evolved again.

Alex continued to stare at me. "You were trying to do things on your own, because you thought you were powerful enough. You thought you could stop him from interfering in the lives of people you cared about. Little did you realize, magic has a way of balancing things out. It's nature. You can't control it. We're bound by it."

"I see that now."

"What *did* you really see?" Alex asked.

What I saw was a glimpse into the possible near future. The gateway could somehow be called open, allowing him to pass through. *Him.* Raefield. Alive. He would come here. He would be flesh in front of my eyes and exist in this time. Had I caused it? Had my presence at his estate triggered the catalyst to force open the pathway? No, only an illusion had appeared.

I swallowed hard.

"I'm serious this time. What happened out east?" Alex pressed again.

I took the last sip of my juice. Even Raegan looked distracted. She turned off the television. Her pleading eyes bore into me with intense curiosity.

"Mom was able to work a spell and send me back in time. Not physically, of course, but symbolically. I stood there like a ghost in my own home, watching my mother and father for the first time interact as they did when they were still alive. I even saw myself moving around the grounds of the Victorian home that I used to live in."

"You saw your parents? That's amazing. Oh, Lauren! To see your parents," Raegan said excitedly. "How did they look? How did they act?"

"I couldn't ask for better parents. They were beautiful people—polite, inviting, respected. Good people. They lived and dressed of that era. They seemed . . . happy. Concerned." I drifted back in time, picturing long skirts and puffed sleeves.

"Who else did you see?" Alex asked.

"I saw him. He was in my home. It was just like my family told me. At one time, Raefield was a part of their circle. He was welcomed into their home, or at least allowed to be close enough to my birth parents. He was important to them, for better or worse."

"Evil man once a confidant. How charming. Nothing like keeping your enemies close by," Alex commented. "If that were me, I'd want to take him out right there and then."

"That's the difference between the two of you. If Lauren had actually been there, she would've waited, planned something out and not acted hastily. She wouldn't jeopardize everyone," Raegan said.

I looked down at the ground.

"I'm not so sure about that. I have this feeling our Lauren may be a bit feistier than she's letting us know. What else haven't you told us?" Alex asked.

I knew it wouldn't be a secret much longer. I didn't want to keep it from them. They were my friends. They had an interest and a stake in what I knew. It could affect their lives as well. I moved closer to the couch. I told them about the events starting from the time we settled into the hotel on George Street to the voices that had called me into the bizarre room down the hall. I told them about visiting my former home and the influences surrounding the Queen Anne. The voice had called to me again. I didn't know if she'd meant to help or to harm. I went into detail about my transformation back in time, and I dissected the episodes during which the ghosts of old New Haven might have suspected my presence.

Alex's eyes widened. I knew he wanted to know about Raefield.

"He's more powerful than I ever imagined. How did he know a presence lingered in the room when you went back in time? How did he sense some spirit leaving when he stood there in your parents' room? We need to know more about this man, in order to take him down. We can't have any surprises." Alex quickly stood and started to pace.

"I assume he's as powerful as my parents, just more clever." I thought back to my mother. "There were times when I thought she knew, or at least sensed, I was there. Maybe not."

"We need to find a way to get to him before he can get to us," Alex said.

"There's more, isn't there, Lauren? Why did you come

home early?" Raegan asked carefully.

Alex stopped his pacing and faced me. "Now for the good part."

I took in a deep breath. I felt more like myself again. Replenished, rejuvenated, and back in full form. "On my own, I decided to go to Raefield's estate one night, despite my family's request that I never go there."

"Ah, ha! Couldn't resist the temptation," Alex remarked. "I don't blame you. I would've done the same thing."

"I think I would've gotten reinforcements first and brought along a few tricks, you know, as back up," Raegan added. "This Raefield sounds like pure evil."

"He's no Mr. Nice Guy, but that wasn't my first mistake."

"Here we go," Alex cajoled.

"Shhh, Alex. Hear her out. Go ahead," Raegan encouraged.

"I sort of did something to Quinn, something I'm really ashamed of."

"You did something to Quinn? *What* did you do, Lauren?" Alex asked.

I paused for a long time. I saw the anticipation in my friends' faces. "I . . . I put a sleeping mixture into his drink. I made sure he wouldn't be able to come after me."

"You *drugged* him?" Alex bellowed.

"It's not like that. I didn't mean to. I just wanted him to rest and to not worry about me. It was my problem."

"I can't believe you did that to him," Raegan said, her dark eyes piercing. "You seriously put him out? No wonder he's not talking to you."

"No kidding. I'd be mad at you, too," Alex replied.

"Don't say that guys. I feel horrible. I've apologized to him over and over again. I've explained why I did it . . . to protect him. I would *never* harm him."

Alex laughed. "Good luck on that one. '*Girlfriend drugs boyfriend, in order to save the world, but she can't figure out why he's furious.*" Alex fanned his arm across the air. "I can see the neon signs now."

Raegan laughed hysterically. She rolled back into the couch.

"You guys aren't helping."

She stopped her chuckling. "You're right, Lauren. We're sorry. We should be more understanding of your plight. It's not everyday that your take on *Arsenic and Old Lace* gets botched. Quinn might want a refund." Raegan resumed her tittering.

"Funny, Kilpatrick. Really charming. And I thought you were my best friend."

"Hey, we're sympathizing with you. Although I've got to say, I'm taking Quinn's side this time," Alex commented.

I got up from the sofa. "I'm done with you characters. I'm going to shower and start my day, or rather my evening." I walked toward the staircase.

"We're here for you. Everything will work out. Quinn has to forgive you," Raegan called out from the couch. "Let's put a movie in," she told Alex.

I ignored my friends. I checked my messages again. "Darn it." At least the night would soon be over by the time I finished. I could catch up on some reading, work on my music, which I'd neglected—thanks to Professor Sobel for giving me time off—or study a little more magic. The music scores and the hefty books could wait. My hidden talents needed to be cultivated and trained. If Quinn wouldn't be here to give me any input, then I'd train on my own. I stared at my door for the longest time.

Forget it, Lauren.

I brushed away the thoughts that kept me at loose ends. *Just wait*, I said to myself again. I reached into the safe haven that housed my magic box. For some reason, I needed to examine the outside again. A nagging feeling suggested that the original design might be different than I remembered. Significance waited to be revealed. I searched and I probed, and I turned the box to every possible angle, but I failed to find any changes.

"The Coming Storm."

If only the message would reveal itself. I had thought it meant Raefield would come through the great, blue mist. Now, I sensed that the message could mean anyone or anything. We needed answers. Soon.

The West Virginia people circled my mind. The words deranged and psychotic floated from Alex's mouth when he spoke about his experience out east. His captivity had been long enough to witness a menacing branch of our kind. Were they any worse than Raefield and company? At least in their defense, they had been born as an aberration to the original design we lived today. It's hard to fight nature, even one as powerful as us.

My thoughts drifted back to Connecticut and to the people I had seen. I saw myself in the garden again, in the sun-filled day of late summer without the heaviness of what lurked ahead. Everything sang and everything bloomed. I had walked the grounds. I had walked toward him. He'd found me. His face glowed and welcomed me. He waited for me, standing under the sunlight as real as I remembered, like I had been lost for a very, very long time.

Oh, Quinn!

Somewhere, the image changed. Darkness came, and then

loneliness took its place. Something beautiful slowly left me, replaced by an aching heart. I stood in front of my Victorian home. I couldn't go to it. I couldn't go to the people inside who needed me. I reached out for them in my attempt to stay. All I saw was that man, who laughed at me as he stood framed in the window. . . .

And fire.

Fierceness shook me. I jumped up and searched the darkened room. I remained in my bedroom, but nightfall covered the dim light from my window. Had I fallen asleep thinking about the past? It wasn't a dream. I had lived there, and I had gone back. My head started to clear.

It's late.

The clock beamed 2:00 am. I couldn't fall back to sleep like I normally did. Something was missing. My body called out to me, a deprivation I knew too well.

I glided down the staircase. My feet moved like the air. The night light in the living room glimmered in the darkness. A soft and eerie presence resonated throughout the house. Raegan slept on the couch, Alex sprawled on the floor like a campground had been set up. I maneuvered around them and made my way into the kitchen. I reached inside the fridge for a bottle of cold water and drank it down in seconds. For a moment, it seemed to satisfy my thirst. I could go back to sleep knowing I overcame.

Then, it happened. That strange feeling of something aching and something missing returned. My sole companion kept me awake on this very long night, which demanded my full attention. I couldn't escape it. But what had gone missing? The shadowy kitchen and all its neat compartments appeared unchanged. I followed what remnants of light danced in the room from the outside world. A reflection of light lingered in my inviting yard.

Following the glow into the damp yard, I traced its origins as it grew larger from where I stood. I knew where it led. The yellow light glowed brightly in that familiar room. It appeared high as a tower to call me home. I suddenly realized what I could fix. There, he stood as he had before, representing what had become lost. I felt happy again. I would go there again.

I continued to look deeper into the window. It began to change. His image became distorted. Where was that pleasant silhouette? I looked up again. The window shifted. Confusion rose. The shadow turned into something ugly. . . .

I closed my eyes to shut out the disturbing image. I didn't want to see. When I looked up again, the light faded away.

"*Nooo!*" I reached out.

The void came back strong. The aching and empty feeling washed over me again, as if it had never left. I knew exactly what he meant the last time that I saw them. She had known, too.

I couldn't breathe anymore. The natural air that filled my lungs felt trapped. I couldn't fix what had gone missing, because I could never go back and see them again. The ground suddenly shifted beneath my feet. I felt myself falling. The emptiness inside would take over.

Accepting what I couldn't change.

A familiar arm reached out for me. "*Lauren,* what are you doing out here?" Raegan grabbed me before I reached the ground. "You're so cold. Let's get inside before it downpours." The drops of rain felt good on my face.

I followed Raegan like a lost puppy. She put her arms around my shoulder to keep me warm. This felt real. I looked up at the window again. The light flickered like a candle, but no one stood in the shadows. Raegan pulled me forward. I continued into the house, now fully awake, but all I heard was the sound of laughter.

*

My eyes opened instantly to the warm, penetrating sun coming through the curtains. Another day. A new day arrived. Last night blurred my senses as I recalled standing outside and staring at the window. Had I really seen the image change? I shook my head. I quickly got myself ready and hurried downstairs.

"Raegan, I think we could get into that class today, I'm sure they'll let. . . ."

"Lauren . . . you're up. I was about to check on you," Raegan said, surprised.

I stopped at the base of the staircase. I stared at the person who stood ten feet away from me. The knot in my stomach returned.

"Quinn just stopped over to see how we're all doing. Isn't that nice of him, Lauren?" Alex remarked. "Maybe we can all have a nice lunch sometime and reminisce about the old days. Or, we can get Quinn up to speed about what's going on after the silent treatment gets lifted." Raegan pinched him hard on the arm. "Hey! Can't a guy be encouraging?"

"We'll be at Alex's place. And we'll be out for a long time." She grabbed her keys and purse, pulling Alex by the sleeve.

The room felt deathly silent. I didn't know what to say. I didn't know what he'd say. We just stared at each other, surprised and cautious. Then, I looked away.

"You look good. Well-rested," Quinn began. "I mean, settled in from the trip. Being back home does wonders."

I thought he'd be annoyed, but his face appeared gentle and kind. "I'm glad we're back. I've had plenty of opportunities to sleep, more than usual. That's what Raegan told me." I hesitated, unsure to take any further steps.

Quinn relaxed. "She noticed. She was the one who came over. She wanted me to see you."

"Oh." I took a step back.

"I'm glad she did. I meant to see you sooner, but I wanted to clear my head. All of this traveling has made me restless. I feel like I haven't stopped traveling since I arrived to the present day." He extended his hand to me. "It's good to be back."

I clasped his hand, weaving our fingers together. Familiar and warm. "That's understandable. It's been a pretty wild ride for you going from coast to coast. It doesn't seem to end."

"I don't mind. It's for a good cause."

My guilt surfaced again. "Look, Quinn, I'm sorry about every—"

He raised his hand. "You've already said enough. I know you feel bad. I didn't come here to give you a lecture, and I'm not here to make you feel guilty. I'm sure you can do that all on your own. Maybe now you can stop putting all the burden on your shoulders."

"But it was wrong and selfish."

"Yes, but it was human. I keep forgetting that about you. I see a perfect person—kindness, beauty, power, and strength—a true witch to the core. A part of me assumed you'd do everything right and know what to do—like a seasoned pro. Poor judgment on my part. Somehow, I became blinded to your flaws. But that's just it. You're also human, and that makes you perfect. So, no, I'm not angry with you."

He drew me closer into his arms. I made sure to stay there. I didn't want to let go. "Better?" he whispered.

"I'll tell you later. Let me have this moment."

Whatever affect I seemed to have on him, I suddenly found myself reciprocating the kisses he planted on my head, my cheeks, the jawline near my ears, and then to my waiting lips. It seemed like forever since I'd felt his touch. It wasn't dull or routine, but new and familiar at the same time. I thought I had lost him completely. I pulled him even closer.

Quinn grabbed the blanket from the couch, shook it out, and arranged it on the floor. We both dropped to our knees, our lips still locked. Something awakened inside of me. Quinn kissed me even more aggressively. His strength kept me from feeling lost again. His hand skimmed beneath my shirt, running his fingers along the contours of my ribs, and then across my midriff, seeking the familiar places he knew so well. I remembered his touch. He kissed me tenderly in all of those places that longed for his touch.

"Don't ever leave me again," I whispered.

"Not a chance," he murmured.

Quinn moved his hands across my legs. Electrical currents sped across my body like wildfire. The darkness lifted from me. Lasting energy prevailed. Every cell in my body felt recharged. Quinn's kisses turned urgent, and I reciprocated. I stopped searching for that missing part, because it had never left. I couldn't wait any longer, and he knew. We moved in unison to the calls of lost and lasting love. I felt free. I only wanted more. My hands grabbed the blanket tightly until I couldn't hold on. Then, I let go. All of my energy released outward, then slowly came back to my core and allowed my heart and lungs to return to its steady pace. I gently kissed Quinn on the lips.

"Hi," he said.

"Hi, again."

We both lay quietly on the blanket for a fair amount of time, Quinn wrapped around me. His face pressed against my neck. I closed my eyes. Peace surrounded us.

I suddenly pulled away.

"What is it?" he whispered, still holding onto me.

"What did Raegan say to you?"

"You want to talk about it *now?*"

"Umm . . . yeah, if you don't mind."

Quinn frowned. "Let me clear my head." We both got dressed and sat down on the couch.

"She came over with as much sincerity and respect for your feelings so as not to invade your privacy. Bottom line, she insisted that I talk to you."

"She didn't have to beg."

"She didn't. She was very straightforward. It was more in the line of 'whatever is going on between the two of you, and whatever really happened in Connecticut, you need to put that aside, because she needs you even if she doesn't say it' sort of speech."

Leave it to Raegan to come forward when it's important. Quinn must've been surprised.

"I wasn't ignoring you." He moved in closer. "A misunderstanding isn't going to scare me away. We've been through enough. We're time-tested."

I chuckled. Everything on this end felt right again. For now. I couldn't ask for more. My thoughts returned to Raegan. "Finish what she told you."

"She told me about last night. Do you remember it?"

"Vaguely . . . well, sort of. It's distorted and clear at the same time."

"Why were you outside?"

I hadn't thought about it much today. "I just woke up. Something bothered me. I had a hunger that I couldn't control, so I went downstairs to the kitchen, thinking I was thirsty or hungry. But it wasn't that. After I lingered in the kitchen, I was pulled to a reflection outside. It came from your room."

Quinn looked puzzled.

I hesitated. "Were you standing there?"

"At the window last night? No." Quinn narrowed his eyes. "You thought it was me?"

"My mind played tricks. The image and light came from your room, so I assumed it was you. At least, it started that way."

"Then, what?"

"The image became distorted. It changed into something else." I turned away, feeling lost again.

Quinn paused, then said, "It was him like the last time you saw him when you left old New Haven during that spell your mother performed. Why would you be getting this message?"

"I don't know, maybe it was some nasty reminder that he'd planned everything behind the scenes. That he held the advantage."

"Because. . . ."

"Because last night it hit me. It would be the last time I could go back there. I won't have that moment again. I won't be able to see them," I finally said. I took in a deep breath and held my anger and grief inside. I felt nothing. I couldn't afford that luxury. "And in the twisted image, I remembered his smug face. He knew I couldn't stop what would happen."

Quinn looked sympathetic. "I'm sorry, Lauren. For

everything. To have to be constantly reminded of the painful realization that you can't change what happened, and to have Raef looming in the background just isn't fair."

"Nothing's fair. It's *my* reality."

Quinn reached for me again. "But you're not alone. Remember that. Your family and your friends are with you. *I'm* with you." He planted a much-needed warm kiss on my lips to remind me of all that I possessed.

I abruptly let go of him.

"This again?" Quinn asked, annoyed. He refused to move away.

"There's something else."

"What is it?"

I didn't know how to say it, but he had the right to know. "I think she knew."

"Who knew?" Quinn asked, puzzled.

"Eden. She knew I stood in the garden."

Quinn's eyes doubled in size. A storm of thoughts and flashbacks of yesterday most likely played through his mind. *"She knew?* I mean, the two of you . . . you both shared a connection?"

"I didn't realize it at first, but before she went into the house after talking to you, she knew I was standing there. I felt a connection, and I'm sure she felt it, too," I explained to him. "I saw it in her eyes. She knew I had come. She knew we could never be here again."

Quinn appeared mindful.

"I don't think she realized what would happen, but I think she knew something horrible would take place. She sensed that my presence conveyed a serious message to her, and she knew it would be the last time."

Quinn slumped back onto the couch. I saw the questions

that roamed through his thoughts. Then, he straightened up. "So, Eden knew. You knew."

"Correct."

"It's so mindboggling. She saw her future self come back to the past in order to warn her of an impending future. That's pre-emptive," Quinn said.

"Yeah, try being the two main characters."

"Why didn't she tell me?" Quinn asked.

"I guess we have our reasons, but since I don't remember, I can't tell you what they were," I responded thoughtfully. "Did you feel anything?"

"I guess now that we're talking about it . . . maybe. I mean, it was so long ago. I felt something strange or out of place, but I didn't know it was you." Quinn's thoughts drifted again. "You were upset about something. I thought it was all the plans we were making and the coming of the new century." His eyes softened.

I was afraid to ask him if we ever married. I no longer existed as the Eden he'd known, or whom he'd planned to make a home with at the Maxwell Inn.

Quinn intercepted my thoughts again. "It was an exciting time for us, but you felt disturbances, something not right in the energy. You even told me if something happened to you—"

"My love is always with you," I said, repeating the words in the present.

Quinn smiled. "Then, Eden . . . you knew something might happen. If I had known it was really you."

"You couldn't. The connection needed to be exceptionally strong, like a person divided into two identical beings. We were momentarily split, and that was enough to ignite that kind of supernatural event."

"You thought he knew you couldn't stop events from happening when you saw him in the window. That would mean Raefield knew you were there?"

"I don't know. There were times when I watched him and my mother interact in the great room that I thought he sensed some kind of presence, or my presence. Before I left New Haven, I thought he knew it was me. Now, I'm not so sure. And just like my birth mother, I thought she knew I stood before her."

Everything was now out in the open for Quinn and I to analyze. Secrets no longer existed between us, only my lost memory held crucial details that tied everything together. It would have to wait for now.

"Since we're exchanging stories, I'm sorry I did that to you. I wasn't trying to get even. I thought you could use the much-needed rest," Quinn explained.

8

THE GETAWAY

I kept to my usual routines. I went to work, I studied my music with Professor Sobel, and I spent time with Quinn and my friends. I also managed to have the usual dinners at my parents' place. Nothing really changed. The adventures in Connecticut existed behind the closed doors of my mind. My family didn't talk about our excursion, and they managed not to argue about my best interests. Once Cameron and Gavin found a nice apartment on the north shore of campus, where they could easily blend in and avoid suspicion, our reinforcements improved.

"What classes did you sign up for?" Cameron asked me. "Gavin signed us up for all senior level courses. He wants to be done sooner. I'd like to stay for the duration, you know, get the full college experience. I think I'm going premed."

"That sounds like you. I'm taking a few accelerated classes, but I still don't know what I really want to do. By sophomore year, they want you to decide on a major," I replied.

"*School?*" Alex called out. "How can you guys be so focused on school? I just do what I need to do to get by. The rest is all going towards the study of life—like survival."

"What would you have us do, hang around at home and do nothing? Being in school keeps us blended in. Besides, I kind of enjoy academia," Gavin proudly answered.

"How can you blend in when your goal is to finish college in two years? *That* might attract attention," Alex retorted.

"I can't help it if I'm bored. School isn't difficult. It's not like I advertise it."

"Why don't you try working at the mall, or a coffee shop, or in construction instead of proving what you can excel on paper? Be one with the populace," Alex suggested.

"Because, my friend, when you're class valedictorian, people expect you to succeed. If I didn't go to college, it would raise some eyebrows," Gavin responded.

"Platteville is a small town. Any yahoo can do well," Alex remarked.

"Can you?" Gavin asked.

"I don't have to try. It just comes naturally."

"Guys, guys. Do we really need to fight over whose methodology is the best way to avoid suspicion?" Justin said. "Isn't it enough that we're always subconsciously looking over our shoulders for undesirables? I say live your life to the best that it can be lived, without drawing too much attention. We knew this would happen, and we knew we could be a target to anyone—human or wizard."

"I, for one, always knew that being a witch meant always being prepared," Elsie added. "Nobody asked us if we wanted this. Nobody gave us a laid out plan and explained our purpose. But I don't care. I don't mind being different."

Alex and Gavin stopped debating. They brushed off their differences.

"I'm with you, Elsie. Before I knew who I was, I always felt different from other people. Now that I know, I'm enjoying this added dimension of myself. It's taken some getting used to. It does have it's drawbacks—case in point always being a constant target—but I could never have this type of bond with you guys or my family or Quinn if we weren't so *different*," I admitted to my friends.

"Well, I wouldn't have it any other way. You guys are more fun than normal people. And I get to have my circle of bodyguards," Raegan chimed in.

"And more danger around you," I mumbled.

"*Pshaw!* I can handle it. Nobody is after me. I get to see everything and still be hidden."

"Anyone even comes close to you, I'll take him out," Alex interjected, putting his arm around Raegan.

"That's what I mean," she replied.

"Okay, okay. Now that we've all had a heartfelt moment and everyone has opened up about their feelings, let's get out of here," Cameron said.

"You're just bitter because you haven't found someone," Alex teased.

"Statistically speaking, the likelihood of any of us having a lasting relationship is pretty slim given the history of Raefield's determination. When he's after someone, he usually finds a way to destroy that person or the people in his or her life," Cameron pointed out.

"Well, that's pretty grim. Whatever happened to living a full life? Put that into your equation," Alex stated.

"I'm just speaking statistically. I didn't say it was definite."

"Yup. Sounds bitter to me," Alex responded matter-of-factly.

"Okay, guys. Why don't we go do what we came here to do and let the future decide for us? I vote with living a meaningful life," I said to everyone.

"I'm with you, Lauren. Let the boys squabble over who's right. The women will take care of everything as we always do," Elsie said. She grabbed Raegan and I by the arms and led us out of the house. The rest of the group followed behind us, a few snickering comments in parting.

"*Woof, woof.*"

"Go back inside, Oscar, and watch over the house. Get anyone who seems suspicious," Raegan ordered. Alex closed the door after Oscar ran inside. Keeping the dog safe meant locking him in the house.

"So, what is this place?" I asked.

"It's a little hideaway we found. Leave it to the men to have foresight," Alex commented.

"Actually, Justin, Elsie, and Cameron stumbled upon the place. Justin and Alex have been setting up the loft for all of us. I've only been there a few times," Gavin explained.

"You'll like it, Lauren. It's a good place to practice," Justin stated.

Justin, Cameron, and Gavin climbed into Cameron's truck and the rest of us crowded into Raegan's BMW. I knew my friends wouldn't sit around and forgo preparations. Like Elsie said, we should always be prepared.

"Where is this mysterious place?" I asked my friends as we headed south down Western Avenue. We passed Rosehill Cemetery on our left.

"You'll see. It's closer to the city. If everything works out, we'll be spending more free time there," Alex said from the front seat of the car.

"It was sheer luck that we found the place. I'm sure you've been to West Town," Elsie stated.

"Yeah, I know the area, but I haven't been down there in a while. There are some popular places and some transient areas in West Town. This should be interesting." I focused on the passing landscape.

We crossed the 90. We then reached the outskirts of where my friends planned to take me. Leave it to Raegan to speed and get us to the surprise. From what I had heard, this area had gone through its heyday, only to fall into a decline. Today, though, I noticed an old world mixing with an emerging new one.

"We're almost there," Elsie said.

"The East Ukrainian Village? How original," I commented. "Have you and Justin been decorating?"

"If you call setting up a gym, weapons room, and sorcery home décor—sure," Alex replied.

"I know I'm excited," Raegan said, parking her car. She got out first, her red hair pulled back into a ponytail and sporting tennis shoes. "I'm ready for my lessons."

"Hold on, pretty thing. You're here to watch until we get a handle on the exercises. If this is Lauren's first workout, I'm sure we'll see things shaking and flying. I'd rather have you wear a helmet and some padded gear," Alex cautioned. "In fact, I'm planning on standing clear of her aim."

"I'm not that bad. I have more control than you think."

"We'll see about that. One never knows with you reinvigorated witches. A stone is a powerful thing," Alex said.

"The others are here. Let's get inside. We should have enough energy for a good workout," Elsie said. She led us to the iron door, which was bolted with a chain lock around the handle and a sliding metal latch that opened up with a combination code.

"Keeping everyone in?" I asked.

"Keeping undesirables out," Elsie replied.

Justin, Gavin, and Cameron joined us. "I've got the key," Justin said as he reached into his backpack and removed the oversized key. He unlocked the iron door and slid it aside to reveal the room behind its protective wall. He flipped on the switch from the electric box located on the right. "Welcome to the loft."

We stared at the open room in awe. A second floor with a balcony surrounded the loft. The building appeared higher than two stories, resembling an abandoned warehouse. Painted stone walls and plenty of room to workout.

"This is nice. You guys went all out," I said.

"Just call this our second home, a small retreat away from the norm," Justin said. "I have three keys—one for you and Raegan, one for Gavin and Cam, and one for the rest of us. The place is solid. Noise doesn't travel, and the building doesn't stand out."

"Let's get started. We have a lot of ground to cover," Alex mumbled.

"Gavin, Cam, and I set up the security inside and around the perimeter, and Alex wired the station to that corner," Justin said, pointing to the sophisticated equipment already set up. The computer nerve center lit up on command. "We can still sense a wizard approaching, even behind these heavy walls. When no one is here, the place is constantly being monitored in and around the loft."

"Very nice. You guys thought of everything." I turned to the fitness area.

"Leave it to the men to get things done," Alex said in a snarky voice.

"Here you have your standard punching bag, and over there you have your blades, knives, and sharp instruments. Weapons may come in handy if all else fails," Justin said somberly.

"We've set up ropes above the ceiling to practice acrobatic moves. We can't solely rely on the ability to move quickly, especially when flying through the air during an attack. Having the agility to conform and rebalance yourself will be critical for your next move," Cameron pointed out. He led us over to the kitchen. "Here you have a basic kitchen. It's stocked with some food for fuel and, of course, a few useful concoctions. I think everyone should dig up their family recipe and share it with the group."

Everyone voiced their agreement.

"Last, but not least, the floor mats are used to practice the ways of attack, defense, and softening the blow just in case you lose your balance and need a soft landing." Alex turned to Raegan with a serious but gentle tone. "I'm asking you this time to stay out of the way for your own good."

"I promise," Raegan replied.

"What's up there?" I asked, pointing to the rooms situated off of the balcony.

"It's just like an apartment. There are four bedrooms. If any of us had to move, and move quickly, we'd have a place to stay. It's secure and it's closer to the city. Leaving town is the other option," Justin explained.

We split into two groups to start the workout. Our craft.

"We know we can do the big things . . . bring on fire, a storm, make the ground shake. But this might help it last. The witch from Clam Lake gave us these herbs. She said that, when we throw it into the air, the spell in motion can give us longevity. That should help slow any adversaries and keep us from losing too much energy," Gavin explained. "I haven't tried it out since there hasn't been reason to waste the stuff. I'm sure it'll eventually come in handy."

"Okay, Lauren. We know when you concentrate, that

mind of yours can throw a good punch. But how quick are you?" Alex asked. He charged at me.

"Lauren, get out!" Raegan called out.

I already anticipated Alex's move the moment his feet went into motion. I turned the bracelet and disappeared. Not even a vapor lingered where I stood. Alex charged the air.

"Wow, Lauren! Where are you?" Raegan exclaimed.

"Two can play that game," Alex challenged. He turned his gold ring. A second later, he vanished into the invisible world. "I can see you now."

I made myself reappear as I took a few steps away from my attacker. He did the same thing and moved closer to me.

"Now what do you do?" Alex demanded as he charged at me again.

Instinctively, I leapt out of the way and into the air, doing a summersault then twisting my body so it turned another direction. I now faced his back.

"Pretty good," Alex said.

"I've been practicing with Quinn and Dr. Sendal."

"And what if I did this?" Alex opened his palms out.

I knew what came next. He sent an energy surge in my direction. My defenses instinctively went up. I blocked the charge coming toward me . . . and the other one and the next one until he gave up.

"Is that all?" I sent my own current in his direction before he could send the next one out.

"Ouch! Lauren, that stings," Alex bellowed out, reaching for his left leg.

"Two *can* play that game."

"All right, all right, you've made your point." Alex turned to the others. "Hey, you guys, come over here. Let's see how far Lauren can go."

"I'm not so sure we should do that," Justin cautioned. They moved closer to us.

Raegan's eyes were glued to us as she moved further away. "Alex, maybe you shouldn't be so hard on Lauren."

"It'll be fine. We need to see what she can do. It's the only way," Alex said.

"Alex is right. I have to be ready for the worst," I replied grimly.

"Everyone, come around her. We won't push it . . . at first, but we have to make her draw it out," Alex directed. My friends did what they were told. They surrounded me and made me feel like a caged animal.

"No hard feelings, okay, Lauren? This is just practice," Cameron said, looking embarrassed.

"We won't try so hard," Elsie said, her voice slightly shaking.

"You have to. Lauren is the target, and she may be the last one standing," Alex insisted. "Everyone focus on her, starting with me and Justin."

I felt my two friends sending the charged power at me. I was ready. I put up a wall of steel. Their energy only tapped at my protective layer. My friends continued to hurl their electricity at me.

"Now, Gavin, Cam, and Elsie, attack her, too!" Alex ordered.

I felt a slight weakening of my defenses, but I refocused my energy into protecting myself once I calculated the growing amount of energy directed at me. I pushed aside their daggers. It bounced off the invisible wall I'd set up.

"Focus everyone. Now push it. Concentrate all of your energy on Lauren," Alex commanded.

"Are you sure? What if we hurt her?" Cameron called out.

"Just do it!" Alex bellowed.

Their will pushed against mine, penetrating through my protective layer. I felt myself slowly lowering onto the ground. My invisible wall closed in. I couldn't believe how weak I became.

Focus, Lauren!

"She's getting weaker!" Elsie yelled out.

"C'mon, Lauren! You have to do better! *Concentrate! Use it!"* Alex shouted.

And just when I thought their energy could physically harm me, the room began to shake.

"Whoa, whoa! What's going on?" Raegan cried out. "Lauren, are you doing this?"

Everything lit up inside. My dormant power suddenly charged alive with life. My head felt cleared and focused.

"Lauren, your eyes," Raegan muttered.

"That's our Lauren. Keep going everyone. Keep pushing it!" Alex exclaimed.

I moved forward. I stopped being defensive and pushed my energy at all five of my friends. It rattled their defenses. Alex was the strongest, so I focused more of my powers onto him.

A sense of excitement moved through me.

"Get ready, everyone!" Alex announced.

The energy continued to soar; it moved beyond my will. The gem worked in synergy with my own powers to add an unparalleled force. A turn of events then took place, which increased my powers. When I encapsulated my opponents, I drew out their powers temporarily.

"What's going on?" Gavin asked, eyes wide. "Where are my powers?"

"Oh, oh. Now we're in her web," Justin said in a nervous tone.

"Is this what you were getting at, Alex?" I demanded. Instead of disarray, the room now quivered in a controlled rhythm.

"What else can you do?" His reply reminded me of the cheerful manner of a child at an amusement park.

I focused and worked my mind's cunning abilities. My friends became my captives, and they couldn't even move their arms. "Why don't I try this?" I closed my eyes and looked deeper inside, into my own nerve center. I brought the energy completely out into the open. My frightened friends levitated off the ground.

"Oh god, oh god. We're moving!" Cameron called out.

My friends floated high in the air at the level of the second floor.

"Yes! I knew she could do it!" Alex beamed.

"Um, Alex. What if she drops us?" Gavin asked nervously. He turned to me and said, "Don't drop us, Lauren. We didn't mean to attack you."

"So, Alex. Do you want to pad the walls, too?" I asked him, looking up at him dangling from the air. I was certain my green eyes looked blinding and methodical.

"This is so cool. You pulled it off! You pushed yourself!" he congratulated me.

I kept my friends dangling for a few more moments while I admired my strength from a distance. They were safe in my reach and protected by my care. I slowly reversed the flow of powers by transporting their energies back to them.

Steadily, I brought them back down to the floor.

"That was amazing, Lauren! You're the best!" Elsie cheered.

I looked at her and felt the pride swell through me. All the confidence and assurance I had gained resonated through me. We could win this battle.

Cameron moved closer to me. He now appeared composed. "I wasn't scared. I had all faith in—"

"What's happening?" I took a step back. The ground seemed to move.

"*Lauren*, your ears are bleeding!" I heard Raegan call out.

I ignored her warning. Everything spun in the room. I reached for her hands and missed. Darkness covered my eyes and my body felt extremely light.

I drifted.

What I remembered next was the feeling of arms supporting my back.

9

FAMILY HEIRLOOMS

"She's starting to come around," Raegan mumbled.

"Lauren, you're back. We were really scared. We didn't know," Elsie said carefully.

I lingered in a daze. I remembered elevating my friends in the loft. I felt myself gathering powers I didn't know I possessed. Then, Raegan warned me of blood coming out of my ears. I felt lost. Soon, darkness took over. I fell into an abyss.

"Quinn, you're here," I mumbled.

"I'm right here. You're home again. Just take it easy." He put a cup to my lips. "Here, drink this."

I did as he requested. It tasted good and familiar. In a few seconds, I saw everyone clearly.

"Hey, Lauren. Guess I missed all the fun," Noelle said in her usual soft voice.

"You should've been there. We had quite the adventure," I joked, getting up from the sofa in my living room. The dizziness disappeared. All of my friends, Quinn, and Garrett gathered around me. Quinn looked relieved. Alex appeared distant.

"I had to work extra. My parents won't be able to cover

as much of my school expenses as they had planned," she said. "Everything's tight."

"We'll fill you in, but I don't think we'll be doing more of those exercises anytime soon," Elsie said.

Alex approached us from his corner. He appeared lively again. "I don't think today should deter us from trying this again."

Quinn did a double take. "Now wait a minute, Alex. Did you not hear what I said earlier?" he snapped.

"Yeah, loud and clear. Like I had forgotten my hearing aids. I said I was sorry," Alex retorted, gritting his teeth. "She's fine. Look, she's herself and all perky."

A storm reflected from Quinn's eyes. "She's very lucky she's not still out. You have no idea what that type of challenge can do to her." He glared at Alex, then turned away. I thought he might punch Alex in the face. Quinn took a deep breath, his anger capped. "Yes, Lauren is strong. She can handle quite a lot, more than the rest of us. But she's not fully experienced. She hasn't conditioned her body and her mind to work with that magnitude of force against her. She needs to be prepared. She has to understand how to balance that weight and defend herself, otherwise an attack like that, even simulated, could kill her. A morning brunch is not going to do it."

Except for Alex, my friends looked guilty and ashamed. They couldn't face me.

"Really, Quinn, I'm okay. It's not their fault. I agreed to it without thinking. I wanted to know how far I could go. Again, careless and reckless on my part. We won't do that again," I pleaded with him. I reached out to him.

His eyes softened. "You just can't burn yourself into the ground like that without knowing the consequences. We don't know enough about the stone to take any chances." He gave me a serious look this time. "Draining five people of their powers simultaneously? That's suicide. I don't think even your parents could pull that off. Just keep the training steady."

Justin looked up at Quinn remorsefully. "We promise it won't happen again."

"It was stupid, and we would never harm her. She's our friend," Gavin said convincingly. He turned and glared at Alex again.

Alex just ignored him.

Garrett, who was never quiet and observant, approached Quinn and patted him on the back. "Way to look out for her. She looks sound to me."

"I wouldn't do any less," Quinn replied.

Garrett studied me with curiosity. "How did you do it?"

I thought about it for a moment. "It wasn't really that hard. Not really. More like a juggling act."

Quinn rolled his eyes and tried not to interrupt, but I saw the interest in his gray eyes. My other friends moved in closer.

"I knew the energy came at me, but I wasn't sure how much force it would be until I felt two people throwing their weight at me. I had it under control. When the others attacked me, I could feel their strength, but I was able to shift that energy and put up a fight. Only when everyone used all of their powers did I feel myself start to weaken. I thought I would collapse," I explained. I recalled that sudden feeling of weakness. "But then it happened. The rock inside of me lit up."

"Yeah, we saw it in your eyes," Raegan replied, her excitement soaring.

"I thought it would consume me, and I would lose control. But that wasn't the case. It felt different this time. It seemed to communicate with me. I was in sync with the rock, and we worked together. It knew what I wanted. It listened to me. It *obeyed* me."

"Sounds like you were in the driver's seat this time," Garrett commented. "Looks like Lauren is finally taking control." He looked over at Quinn.

"It doesn't mean she can always control it," Quinn said, his tone flat, shadowed with worry.

"But it's a start. Look, Quinn, I'm not trying to undermine your reasoning, but if she can command the rock instead of the other way around, she's got a fighting chance."

"Sure, that's what I want. What about what happens afterwards?"

"Oh, that," Garrett muttered.

"If we can find a way that doesn't drain her, I'll feel much better. In the meantime, go easy on the super, superhero stuff," Quinn suggested.

"Guess I know what I have to work on next."

＊

Quinn and I haven't spoken about the incident again. We managed to practice from time to time without provoking that subject. I even showed him our new state-of-the-art facility. He was wholly impressed. The training continued on a nondestructive level, although the temptation to push myself to the unknown dangled in front of me. I scaled back when Dr. Sendal commented on pushing myself too hard, and when Mom raised a few questions after she noticed my fatigue.

Then, there was school. I delved into my classes and

enjoyed my sophomore year away from the dreaded freshman year. I managed to keep my part-time job at the library and remain involved in my extra curricular activities. Things progressed smoothly. For the first time in a long while, everything felt normal.

I received a text from Mom.

Lauren, stop by the shop after classes.

She usually doesn't ask me to stop over, but since Chelsea was consumed with grad school, she probably needed someone to help her out for a few hours even though she hired a full-time employee to manage the store.

"Hi, I'm Lauren. You must be Billie. Mom is glad you came on board."

"She's great to work for. I couldn't ask for a more flexible and understanding boss. I'm so glad we finally got to meet," she cooed.

"Oh? Has she said much about me?"

"No . . . not much at all. Just that she has two daughters. Of course I've met Chelsea. It's just exciting to meet her family. I'm so grateful to your mother for hiring me, and to meet all the wonderful customers so far. It's been *sooo* rewarding."

I couldn't help notice that Billie dressed older than she looked, more like someone in her fifties instead of her thirties. Her youthfully styled auburn hair and her lack of wrinkles didn't fit the outfit she wore.

"Your mom just stepped out, but she'll be back soon," Billie said.

She did seem sweet and grateful for the job. "Are you from Chicago?" I asked her.

"No, Omaha. I moved here after I got married, but that didn't last. He didn't want to be married any longer."

"I'm sorry to hear that."

"It's not your fault, sweetie. He wanted his freedom," she said. "So, I stayed in Chicago and worked and here I am. I wasn't going to wallow in self-pity. No siree. You have to pick yourself up even when the times are tough. You have to move on and leave the past."

I liked this new person for her simplicity and her kindness. I could see why Billie had left a good impression on Mom.

"Well, I'll be in her office."

"All right. I'll be here, watching the store," she replied enthusiastically, although she seemed a bit preoccupied. "Oh, Lauren, can I ask you something?"

"What is it?"

"Do these clothes make me feel *in touch* with the customers?"

I chuckled at her quirky nature. "Just be yourself. I think you're doing fine."

Mom had neatly organized her office with reference books and catalogs along the back shelf. Chelsea's desk seemed quiet next to my mother's with only a computer and a few pens left in the holder.

The shop door's soft chimes sounded. "I found what I was looking for," Mom said.

"Your daughter is here," Billie replied.

The familiar footsteps approached me. She peeked her head into the office and saw me sitting at her desk. "It suits you," Mom said, closing the door behind her.

"I could get used to it, but I'll let Chelsea have this one."

"Did you meet Billie?" she asked.

"Yes, she seems very nice, and full of energy."

"Very much so. I wasn't sure at first, but she came highly recommended. She's so knowledgeable about books and history, and she goes that extra distance for my customers. She really has been resourceful."

"Hmmm."

"Of course, we did a background check and looked into all her associates," Mom reassured me.

"Guess that covers that. What did you want to see me about?"

Mom fell silent for a moment. She appeared deep in thought. "I wanted to show you this earlier, but I've been working on restoring it as much as possible. Oh, Lauren, it's the only thing I could find!"

"What is it?"

Mom lifted a manila envelop from her leather tote. I expected to see a rare book from the excitement she displayed, instead of some report behind an ordinary folder. She quickly opened up the envelope and handed me photos stored inside picture protectors.

"I went to great lengths to find the right people. Here, they're for you," Mom said.

I looked at the photos, and I couldn't speak. I stared at the familiar faces neatly protected behind the clear sheets. "How did you get these?"

"I had my suspicion that your family's loyal employees may have wanted to leave a few mementos behind before the fire took place. In fact, I won't be surprised if they were the ones who started the blaze."

"But . . . how? Where did you find them? And *why* would they start a fire?" I thought back to the conversation Quinn and I had had at the aquarium.

"This is the irony. I remembered you vaguely telling me back then about a small hiding place that Clara had showed you. You had said it was in the kitchen, so every time we went to New Haven, I searched the kitchen. I never found anything. During this last trip, I looked in the pantry again," Mom recounted, her eyes widened with excitement. "I found a small compartment, but it was empty. I got frustrated and gave up thinking nothing had been left behind. However, I decided to look into that compartment again. I made sure to reach deeper inside the enclosure. This time, my hands found a latch I could maneuver. I didn't know what it did, but I began to move the shelves again. I was able to slide a shelf over."

I looked down at the pictures again. "We were so unprepared. I can't see the worry on my parents' faces. I was so unassuming."

"You didn't know."

"Maybe I did know something," I whispered, thinking back to the vision of Quinn and I in the garden. I turned to the next photo. "And here we are with Nathan and Clara. They must've been wonderful people."

"Very good people," Mom replied.

I smiled warmly at the next photo. "Quinn and I in a formal pose."

"It was a special time for you both."

I thought back to that nagging scene in the garden when we had looked ahead to the future. I shook off the melancholy feeling. I turned to the next photo to see my parents standing in the library. More formal posing. They looked very focused. I then flipped to the last photo, my eyes narrowing at the image. I studied it carefully. Raefield had a slight grin on his face. He stood between my parents. I didn't recognize the two people standing behind them, but I knew this photo had to have been significant to be saved.

"Who were these people?"

Mom frowned. "They don't look familiar to me. I would assume another witch and a wizard, because this was a closed meeting. I've already asked your father and Dr. Sendal. We don't know. Quinn is my last option."

I examined the photo again. "The corner looks ruined, almost as if the photo didn't completely take. I also see thick and thin lines on this side," I said, pointing to the bottom left corner.

"I don't know what to make of it. I assumed it was just the quality of the time," Mom said.

I slid the five photos back into the envelope.

Mom reached into her case again. She pulled out another item wrapped in cloth. "This is yours now."

I opened my other gifts. "Was this hers?"

Mom's voice caught as she nodded. "Yes, it was your mother's."

I studied the black pearl pendant necklace set in a wired, metal fixture. It resembled a nest. The pearl shone a deep onyx. "Her invisibility charm."

"She always had it with her," Mom said.

I unwrapped the next item. "So this is what my father used?" I picked up the metal coin, admiring the polished, platinum charm with a deep emerald jewel imbedded in the center. It was the size of a quarter.

"Given to him when he was young." Mom placed the coin in my palm. "It's an interesting sort of gift. A ring would've been a better choice, but you don't get to choose your device."

I held both items close to me. I didn't care what type of

special trinkets they had owned. They belonged to my parents and that was all that mattered to me.

"And before I give you the last item, I want you to know that I've never come across this until I found it in the pantry." Mom reached into her tote for the last time. She handed me some rolled up papers, which had been secured with a piece of string. "I'm not sure what it all means."

I eagerly unfastened the string and gently opened the fragile papers. My fingers lightly traced the fancy letters.

n a e r e p l e c o d i

Written in my mother's handwriting. She had wanted to tell me something important. Only through secrecy could she pass on something grave.

She had known something! Did she know I had stood in front of her?

"I don't know what she was trying to say," Mom commented. "Perhaps in her wisdom, she devised a secret code."

"Because she suspected not everyone could be trusted," I said, my fears relived.

Why can't I remember?

I moved on to the next piece of writing. Someone else's handwriting.

> *It was as though the sky*
> *had silently kissed the earth,*
> *so that it now had to dream of sky*
> *in shimmers of flowers.*

The air went through the fields,
the corn-ears leaned heavy down
the woods swished softly—
so clear with stars was the night

And my soul stretched
its wings out wide,
flew through the silent lands
as though it were flying home.

"I looked it up. It's been translated from German. It's a von Eichendorff poem. I honestly don't know what special meaning is hidden within this passage," Mom said. She looked just as curious and confused as I did.

I now owned more riddles and hidden messages and clues that I couldn't solve. First the magic box that housed my bracelet, now all this.

It's all connected. It has to be.

And the fire.

"If only she were here to tell us," Mom said.

I nodded. I gathered all my new earthly treasures and placed them with care in my purse. They really were treasures, and I intended to keep them safe, away from grasping hands. I only wish I had time to figure out what they meant. I looked at the calendar on the wall.

The harvest moon.

Mercedes's warning.

Raefield.

"If I figure something out, I'll tell you," I promised, hugging and thanking my mother. "I think I'll pick Quinn's brain."

"Don't be too hard on him."

I sped out the door, barely saying more than two words to Billie. She called out, "It was nice meeting you!"

I jumped into my Prius and drove away from the shop. The days were growing shorter as autumn crept in, but light still persisted before the sun set. Mom would close the shop at seven today since it was Monday. She would go home and tell Dad that the gifts from the past had been delivered. I, on the other hand, drove to my place to begin yet another quest for the truth.

This would be the second time I would probe Quinn's mind. From Dr. Sendal's advice, my approach needed to be different in order to tame his natural defenses from blocking my intrusion. It was imperative, but if it came to it, I knew how to break through. I only hoped I would find sound answers. I readied myself for the task and ate a well-nourished meal.

"Hi. Did you eat yet?" Quinn asked. He closed the door behind me.

"I did. I got some exciting news from Mom today. She asked me to visit her at the store," I said and motioned him to sit on the couch. "She gave me these." I pulled out the jewelry and placed them in his hands.

"Your parents' charms. How did she get them?"

"Guess Mom had been searching the kitchen of my Connecticut home for years, because she remembered I'd told her about a secret compartment in the kitchen that Clara had showed me. She couldn't find anything, so she gave up. During this last visit, she retraced her steps and found the hiding place. Isn't it wonderful?" I asked, feeling excited again.

"Yes, I remember this necklace around Faye's neck and the peculiar coin that your father carried. This is important stuff," Quinn said, admiring my newfound possessions. "They say having all the jewels of the same bloodline, particularly within the immediate family, can be quite powerful. And in your family, that would be stronger than anyone's, including the Reed family." Quinn suddenly looked perplexed. "Does this mean you had their jewels, or had Nathan and Clara retrieved them?"

"Again, your guess would be better than mine.

I didn't care who placed them in the secret compartment. I savored any physical link I had to my Mother and Father. I put my mother's necklace on and placed my father's coin back in my purse. I planned to make a special, hidden strap with a small enclosure for his coin. "There, it's safely kept close to me. I'll never give it up."

"It belongs to you. It won't answer to anyone as strongly as it will to you."

"As strongly?"

"You're the closest blood link next to Helen. I'm not sure how effective it would be for her."

"I see. Familial dominance. Then I have nothing to worry about."

Quinn remained silent. His eyes probed my oversized purse. "What else do you have?" He reached for the envelope corner sticking out of my bag.

I removed the photos and gave them to him. I waited quietly for his response while he slowly flipped through the five sheets. They would have concrete meaning for him, and validation that the past hadn't been imagined. It was quite real.

"I can't believe Helen found these. It seems so long ago since I've seen these photos in your old house. But this one, I've never seen it before," Quinn said, pointing to the one of the two unknown people standing behind Raefield and my parents. "The family photo with Nathan and Clara and the one with you and I were on the table in your room. The photo of just your parents in the library and the one with you and your parents sat on your father's desk in the same library. That, I remember. But this one . . . nope . . . it doesn't ring a bell."

"Mom doesn't remember it, either. And she doesn't know who the other people were. She asked Dad and Dr. Sendal. She thinks it was a closed meeting."

"Really? Even Helen didn't know, but it somehow involved Raefield. Interesting."

I looked at the photo again. Did *I* know who they were?

"I'm starting to wonder if that old house has any other secret compartments," Quinn muttered.

"Me, too. It seems to contain many surprises. Mom thinks Clara and Nathan put the items in the pantry beyond sentimental reasons."

"You think they're behind the fire, too?"

"Mom believes they might've had a role in the fire as a cover up, possibly to protect my family. They likely hid important information for a reason, whether on their own or if they'd been asked just in case something happened. They knew which items would be of value. They would've been the last people there if we didn't survive."

"No survivors or remaining witnesses," Quinn muttered.

"You said it yourself when we were at the aquarium. The fire was very suspicious. I think they hoped we would eventually find this."

"Someone would come back to the house, possibly during that time or in the future. Very clever of them," Quinn praised. He stopped for a moment, his face lighting up. "It was meant for you to find, because you knew about the compartment. Losing your memory was a result of the stone. They wouldn't have known that would happen."

We both looked at the photos again with careful eyes.

"There's gotta be something else," Quinn said.

I reached into my bag and pulled out the sheets. "There is. Take a look at this."

Quinn grabbed the papers from my hand and read them carefully, over and over again. I saw the bewilderment and frustration in his gray eyes. He shook his head.

"N-A-E-R-E-P-L-E-C-O-D-I. I don't know what to say. I don't know what it means. And this poem?" He fell back into the sectional.

"So, you've never seen them before, and I've never shown them to you?"

"No. I would remember something like this," he said. "It seems like a code. And Helen didn't know?"

"No. She hoped you knew the significance of the photos and the meaning behind these confusing messages. Mom thinks my birth parents devised a secret code. This poem is called *Night of the Moon.* It's a von Eichendorff, translated from German. Are you *sure* you don't remember me telling you about them?"

"Let me think again. Maybe you mentioned something you scribbled on some piece of paper. Oh, I don't know. Lauren, I'm feeling drained," he pleaded with me.

I moved in closer. I reached for his gentle face. "Then you wouldn't mind if I take a look."

"I guess we could. Take me while I'm at my weakest," he said, laughing nervously. "I didn't have much today."

"I promise not to hurt you."

My hands gently pressed against his face. My fingers soon

made their way through his unruly hair. He'd let his hair grow out in the past month from the waves caught between my fingers. I felt him start to relax. He seemed to enjoy this foreplay. His eyes closed, and the tightness on his masculine face softened. My job would be easier this time. I then wrapped my long fingers tightly around his forehead and at the sides of his head. Pressing harder against his precious head, his body began to shake as the energy rushed out of me and into him.

"Forgive me, love."

In seconds, I crossed over. It was effortless this time. I now swam in his extensive memory, crossing from one moment to another in record time, yet I never stopped at a single event. I programmed my mind to only search for the letter even though temptation hovered over me to stop at everything he had encountered. I knew I needed to stay focused for his sake.

I suddenly stopped at the only credible scene I found and directed my energy on that moment. Quinn stood in the doorway of an elegant suite. He watched me as I sat at a desk.

"I could feel you coming from down the hallway." I crumpled up a sheet of paper before turning to him. *"I wanted to be ready before you came, but my thoughts were elsewhere. It must be all this planning that has me so preoccupied,"* I said sweetly.

"Then let's not worry. Come, we should take a moment outside and enjoy the day. It'll be here when we return." Quinn reached out his hand.

I followed his lead, slipping one hand into his and the other into the side pocket of my long skirt.

"What has your mind so engaged on that your attention was thwarted and something private was stashed in your pocket?" Quinn asked.

"*Oh, just some ideas about the future. Nothing to worry about.*"

We made it down the stairs and into the main lobby where a crystal chandelier hung high above our heads. The Maxwell Inn.

"*It's chilly out there. Let me fetch your wrap,*" Quinn quickly suggested, fast on his feet. He disappeared.

He unlocked the room and quickly grabbed the cream colored shawl from the bedroom. He reached the door, but he paused and decided to turn around. Something on the desk caught his attention. He overlooked a pile of blank papers covering the middle of the desk, but reached over to a ledge where a decorative bowl sat. He withdrew a ball of crumpled paper from the bowl and opened it.

1 Go
11 Destroy
12 It

Quinn stood in the formal room for a few minutes, reading the passage over and over again. I felt his heavy thoughts. Confusion. Concern.

"*What is she doing?*" he mumbled.

Quinn put the piece of paper back into the decorative bowl and rushed out of the suite. In moments, he reached the lobby where I waited for him.

"*Here, this will keep you warm. We won't be gone for long.*" Quinn wrapped the shawl around my shoulders and also kept his arms around them.

"*What is it?*" I asked.

He removed his arm from around me. "*It's nothing. It's just . . . I want to make sure you understand we're partners—a team. Whatever troubles you, troubles me.*"

"*I know that, love. There is no doubt,*" I said sincerely. "*Let's wash away that frown on your face."* They walked through the French doors and out onto the property where the picturesque bay opened in front of them.

Quinn still wasn't convinced.

"Good day, Mr. Maxwell. Miss De Boers."

"Lovely day, Mr. Maxwell."

Quinn picked out a spot along the greenery and laid out a blanket where he and Eden would sit. He felt concern again. *"Dearest Eden, I don't want to harp about this, but I have a confession. When I returned to the room, I noticed a piece of paper crinkled up into a ball in the bowl above the desk. I suppose it wasn't meant for me to see, but it did catch my eye. Nevertheless, I read what was inscribed on the note. Darling, what does it mean?"*

"A note?"

"Yes, something about 'Go Destroy It'. Can you explain this to me? Should I be alarmed?"

Quinn noticed that my eyes grew larger for only a second and then returned to their normal appearance. My face remained composed. I chuckled. *"Oh, that. It's just some silly game I was playing with Mother. Nothing concerning."*

Quinn looked relieved. *"Good, then we shall have a pleasant morning before lunch and back to work. But before we close this subject, promise me you won't keep any secrets from me. I would like to know if something is wrong."*

"I promise."

"Then it's settled. From now on, you and I will look into the future as family. We won't have to guess. Eden—"

I heard Quinn gasp.

I quickly released him from my grip. He turned weaker than I expected. I jumped up from the sofa and grabbed the first thing I could find in the fridge and rushed it to him. "Here, drink all of this."

Quinn gulped down the entire protein shake in mere seconds. I handed him another one. He drank that one as well, only not as fast. The color and the clarity returned to his face and eyes.

"That was close. I thought I was going under. Everything started to go dark," Quinn said.

I sighed. "Sorry, guess it was a little too much. I thought I was being careful."

"I didn't realize I'd feel this drained. You really don't know your strength." He reached over and crushed the empty shake containers. "Did you find what you were looking for?"

"Not that much, only a few translated words on a crumpled piece of paper. Why don't you tell me about them?"

Quinn got up from the sofa and threw the cans away. He went into the fridge and grabbed two more, then returned to where I stood. "Just in case this gets long."

"I'm waiting."

Quinn chuckled. "I didn't know this was of significance until you came here. As you recalled, you had stuffed it into a bowl, which I accidentally found. Your words were something in the line of 'Nothing concerning'. So, I didn't push the subject."

"That's it?"

"That's all."

I couldn't believe what Quinn told me. After nearly draining his energy, only a few words could be retrieved.

"Now, I should be the one to get it out of you, but since you don't seem to remember, we're both at the same point," Quinn said.

I stayed quiet for a moment. A jabbing sensation around

my heart and a few turns of my stomach prompted me to turn to him, my expression pained. "Except I knew it was something and withheld it from you."

"I'm sure you had good reasons."

"Well, I'm not feeling any better," I blurted out, taking in a deep breath. "What could've been so important that I kept this from you? Were my birth parents trying to tell me something, something so important they wrote it in code? *Destroy what?*" My hands formed a fist in the air. "Geez, Quinn. What was I trying to figure out? What did I know?"

Quinn looked sympathetic. "It's not your fault."

"No, but I had first-hand knowledge. We can both agree on that. See? Look at the handwriting on the poem. It was Eden's—mine. It's the same writing when she scribbled 'Go Destroy It'. I *did* know something."

He looked at the poem again. "I remember it now, the style you used."

"And what did I do? Obviously, not enough."

"We don't know that for sure. Maybe you did do something. Don't be so hard on yourself."

"And this?" I pulled out the photo of the meeting. "Is this related?"

Quinn shrugged his shoulders. He kept his lips tightly shut. It was useless to argue with me when all he saw was a debate I carried on by myself.

"Look, I'm not going to argue with you anymore because it won't change how you feel. *I* believe there was good reason for all of this. And the more I listen to you—and see what's been uncovered—the more I feel that your parents did what they could under the circumstances in times that they felt were turning for the worse. It had to be, so that no one else knew," Quinn rationalized. "The less people involved, the better." His voice sounded clear and confident.

"They knew we might've been compromised." I thought back to my parents, who most likely arranged clues and ideas that only a few had known, even if it didn't make any sense. Nothing could be linked! Quinn's reasoning made sense. My temperamental thoughts cooled down. He didn't need me to badger him anymore with things he didn't know. I wrapped my arms around his shoulders. "Are you sure you want to stick around?"

"Do you really need to ask? This is nothing, Lauren. I'm not going anywhere without you."

"Good, because I won't let you leave."

10

SCHOOL DAZE

I enjoyed being in school again. It took my mind off the impending and unnatural events that lived along a parallel lifeline, which the people around didn't realize could actually exist. I felt normal. Most of my close friends resided near campus, and my former high school friends lived within driving distance. My family was healthy and alive, just a heartbeat away if I needed them. Quinn remained a constant in my life.

I checked the date on my phone: September 14.

Maybe nothing will happen, I thought. *Wishful thinking.* Everything seemed relatively quiet in the meantime.

"—And we've been waiting patiently after contact was made, but still no signs of life can be seen or heard."

"What? Are you talking to me?" I asked, looking over at an annoyed and frustrated Raegan.

"Ahhh, yeah. It's not really fun talking to myself. People will start to wonder."

I scanned the classroom and noticed several people were staring at us. "I can't believe I did that. I remember talking to you and then . . . I don't know."

"No kidding. One minute you're here, the next minute,

you're off to La La Land. Your eyes were wide open—buggy like—and they did seem glassy and distant," Raegan whispered. "What were you thinking about?"

"Was I that out of it?"

"Um, like in a heavy trance. Spill it."

"I don't know really. It wasn't that serious. Being reflective, I guess. You know, thinking how normal and great—"

"It seems to me that Ms. Reed and Ms. Kilpatrick have decided to take it upon themselves to run the class. Perhaps they feel that they don't need to follow along. Is there some insight you'd like to share with us regarding today's lecture?" Professor Williams asked.

"No, ma'am. You have our full attention," I mumbled.

"Ms. Kilpatrick?"

"No, Professor Williams. We're just going over the lecture."

"Good. Since you ladies are thoroughly engaged, perhaps you can set a noteworthy example for the class. I'll expect a summary of Bayes' theorem with an example tomorrow morning on my desk. You can find it in your stats textbook within the first five chapters," Professor Williams said to us. "This doesn't include the prep work for the quiz on Wednesday."

Raegan leaned over and whispered in my ear, "You're doing my homework."

The rest of the class continued without further interruptions and without my mind wandering off into the weeds. The last thing I needed was to be on another hit list.

"See you this afternoon in history," I said to Raegan as we walked out of Leverone Hall.

"At least I don't have to worry about you disrupting the

class and taking me along. The TA's a pushover. He just needs to do the class to get his graduate work done, and I need the pre-reqs."

I smiled at my dear friend. Raegan turned and waved goodbye to me before moving into the purposeful crowd. I savored this normalcy. My friends could live the everyday life of friends, school, work, and this human existence.

I picked up my ringing phone. "Hey, I'm on my way."

I breezed through the University Library and skirted across a pedestrians' path outside of Norris Center to arrive at Pick-Staiger Hall. I had extra time since I only took the minimal credits to stay in and, of course, to maintain as much freedom and leeway as possible, just in case.

"How was class?" I asked Quinn.

"Not bad. I'm actually enjoying school. Declaring myself a business major turned out to be a good thing."

"Well, you've had first hand experience. And with the credits you somehow pulled off—"

"Out of the blue, I was able to slide into my fourth year. Not too shabby for an out-of-towner," Quinn said proudly. "I really didn't have this chance. I was already destined to take over the hotel with my on the job training. The rest was catching up in the books, all this theory and philosophy."

I felt at peace. We found a quiet corner in the open auditorium where the orchestra was rehearsing Dvorak's 6th symphony. The melody sounded soothing.

"You should really take it seriously," Quinn said to me.

"Take what seriously?"

"Your music. This shouldn't stop you from living and pursuing what you love."

"Are you serious? At this time in my life?"

"What's wrong with this time or any time? Lauren, you

can't put everything on hold for the unknown. Nobody knows. You can't sit and wait only to be on constant guard."

"And what's wrong with being ready?"

"That's not what I meant. Of course, being prepared is one thing, but living your life, *this* life is just as important."

I listened to everything he said, but I couldn't fully agree. "That's fine for everyone else, everyone normal and human that's not holding onto a rock which some crazy man wants. Not me. Everything can change in seconds."

Quinn shook his head. "You *are* human, just with added punch. And what's normal? Going to sleep and school and work? You've got that covered."

"I just . . . can't fully get into it."

"Well, think about it. Everyone else wants the chance. Your friends are blending in, and they seem to enjoy it. Look at your family. They're doing everything they've always wanted to do. Just live, and be a part of this life. The past is . . . gone."

I looked into his wishful eyes. "I know. I'll try. You're right. What's done is done. I can't keep looking over my shoulders. I have a good life that's waiting for me with wonderful people. I do miss this." I looked around the hall again. Normalcy. I chuckled. "My parents would be happy if I finally decided on a major."

"Then have no regrets. Don't let them win."

Them—Mercedes and Nicholas and Raefield, and whoever else emerged from inside the phantom blue cloud. I tried to leave the ghosts of yesterday behind, but they insisted on following me. Unfortunately, most of them were real.

The rest of the morning sped by, followed by lunch with Quinn and some of his new friends. I was happy to see him experience the college dream that he'd talked about. His opportunities had been limited since he already worked at his family's hotel. Quinn seemed happy to talk about the past and the great responsibility of running the family business, but he embraced this life. I needed to do the same.

We jumped into Quinn's car and headed for Harris Hall. "There's a small parking lot next to the building. We'll go there," Quinn said.

"How did you get a pass?"

"Connections."

We headed for the afternoon class. Raegan's version of fun included the history of western science and medicine. We took a gamble and enrolled in a class where most of us could be in one place. I was happy with our decision; we could actually experience college in a public atmosphere. Together.

Raegan and Alex sat at a table with Elsie and Justin. Gavin, Cameron, and Garrett stood nearby talking. Their eyes turned to us when we walked in.

"Saved you a spot," Garrett said.

Quinn and I walked to the table on the opposite side of Raegan when the TA showed up.

"Hello, everyone. As you know, I'll be taking over the class while Professor Young is on sabbatical in Guyana. I was told she should be back before the next quarter."

"I wouldn't mind taking a holiday down to South America. It sure beats sitting in this boring class," Garrett said to Quinn.

"I'm sure you could get an excuse for two weeks," Quinn joked.

"And so, if we could all take a look at the slides for this week's lecture. We've covered the herbal remedies introduced by the Native Americans, and the approach toward modern psychiatry by Dr. Rush. He, too, believed in bleeding his patients. We're going to jump to the Civil War and the challenges facing medicine and surgery when dealing with the massive human casualties and diseases. . . ."

Raegan leaned over. "This is the good stuff. Even though it doesn't have to do with animals, they also went through their progressive treatments to come to this day."

"Spoken like a true advocate. I'll know my future pets will be in great hands," I told her.

"Lauren, I think you should get Quinn to take some time off. I think a much needed vaca will do wonders to get us motivated when the second quarter comes around," Garrett suggested.

"Whose us? And why are we taking a trip in the middle of the semester?" I asked.

"Me, of course, and anyone else who's up for fun."

Cameron turned his head sideways. "You guys are taking a trip? Didn't you just go to Connecticut?"

"It's not that kind of trip. That was more like a *search and cease*. This one should be a fun in the sun or festival holiday. Yeah, I can see it," Garrett said.

"What about the Bahamas?" Gavin chimed in.

"I don't know. Hurricane season could be around the corner," Cameron responded, his head still tilted.

"Don't you guys ever stop talking?" a girl seated next to Cameron asked. "He's going to hear you."

". . . And so the lack of resources and sharing of equipment within the crowded tents acted as a medium for disease to spread in an already limited . . ."

"It's a good thing we're sitting in the back. You could take notes for us this week, and we'll rotate each week. That way, nobody will feel left behind," Garrett suggested. She shook her head and laughed quietly before turning her attention back to the lecture.

Garrett said to Gavin, "That's not a bad idea. The Bahamas would be a great place to—"

Suddenly a loud thud and then a crash reverberated from outside. Everyone looked up and around the classroom. The TA stopped talking, waiting for the next disruption.

"What's going on?" Alex asked, turning to Quinn and I. I shook my head.

Another crashing sound resonated, this time of metal crashing and glass breaking.

"I didn't realize they were doing construction in this area," the TA announced. He leafed through his lecture notes. "The school didn't mention any plans for work at this building."

No one responded. Some appeared confused. Suddenly, tires screeched outside.

A student got up from his seat and looked out the window from the second floor. "Hey, someone's car got totaled." A few other students jumped up to see the spectacle.

"Maxwell, isn't that your car?" another student asked.

Quinn, Alex, and Garrett jumped up front their chairs and headed out of the classroom, followed by the rest of us. We came to a halt. We surrounded the lifeless wreckage lying before us. Crushed and leveled, the tires slashed, the hood left open with the engine dismantled, and both ends of the car slammed into by some kind of wrecking machine. A mist coming from the broken engine suggested acid.

"Man, Quinn. I'm sorry about your car," Garrett said.

Quinn fell deathly silent except for the blazing color that

flooded his face. He just stared at the violated car with stormy pewter eyes.

"Hey, guys, look here. Two sets of tire marks going in different directions," Justin said.

"Who would've done this?" Raegan asked everyone standing around the wreckage.

"It's a warning," Alex muttered.

I reached for Quinn's icy hands. "So much for normalcy."

*

Quinn sat silently in the back of Garrett's Audi. His face remained as hard as stone. He wouldn't look at me, only directly at the road ahead. Garrett turned to me for a brief moment, looking solemn before glancing in his rear view mirror at Quinn. Then, he focused on the road.

We stayed until the tow truck hauled his smashed up car onto the truck and carried it away. Quinn managed to say a few words to the truck driver and answered some basic questions asked by the campus police and the city police.

When we got back to the house, Quinn's face relaxed a bit. I knew he wouldn't let down his guard. "Stay put. I won't be gone for long. I asked your friends to come over."

"I don't need a babysitter."

"Just humor me, okay?"

I nodded. In seconds, Quinn and Garrett climbed back into the dark car and sped away, leaving me in the driveway. I looked up at the road again and saw my friends walking down the street. As if on cue, their presence was requested and they followed through.

"Hey, what a crazy day, huh?" Raegan asked.

"Very unexpected," I mumbled.

"Boy, if I were Quinn, I'd be so *pissed off,*" Cameron said abruptly.

"I think he's more than that," Gavin corrected. "Like a loud and deliberate message to scare him and everyone else." Gavin looked at me for a reaction.

"Why don't I throw a bunch of pizzas in the oven and anything else I can find and put it out on the table. I have a feeling it's going to be a long night," Raegan suggested. "Lauren and I still have extra homework to do."

"Good idea. I think storing up sounds in order. I don't want to be caught depleted in any way," Elsie added.

"You're not suggesting we'll be outmaneuvered anytime soon, are you?" Gavin asked her.

"After today's event, I don't think we should second guess anything. That was a surprise attack. We were all there," she reminded everyone.

After we settled into the house and started to eat, I pulled Elsie aside. "Alex and Justin haven't said much since the incident." I looked over at Alex a few times while we ate, but he never met my gaze. He said a few things to Raegan and mumbled a couple words to Justin, which I couldn't make out.

"I know. Alex being quiet is so not like him. He always has an opinion about everything," Elsie whispered to me.

"Guess we'll just wait for his revelation."

I spent the rest of the evening doing homework and writing up the extra assignment for Professor Williams's class—one for me and one for Raegan's in her own words. My friends did their homework or watched TV.

Nearly ten in the evening and I heard a car pull up the driveway. I looked out the window to see Quinn and Garrett walking toward the door. They stepped inside, behaving as though their arrival was pre-planned.

"Sorry it took us so long. We needed to make a few extra stops," Quinn announced to everyone.

"No worries. We thought about camping out here if it came down to it," Cameron replied, his tone indifferent.

"You guys don't have to do that. You've already done enough. I don't need a security team," I told my friends.

Quinn frowned. "We need to watch each other's backs, Lauren. No one goes anywhere alone. This isn't over."

"I don't think we should over do it. I don't want to feel as if they're taking us hostage," I retorted.

"Lauren, it's not to keep anyone a prisoner. Quinn's right. We must be careful. They caught us with our guard down. They knew we were all together, and they still got to us," Garrett justified.

"They, as in Mercedes and Nicholas?" I asked.

"Could be them, but I suspect other people worked for them since none of us felt another witch in the vicinity. It doesn't matter. They sent us a clear message, and we didn't expect it. We're lucky no one was physically attacked. I'm sure that was the point . . . this time," Garrett responded.

Elsie agreed. I knew deep inside they were right. Quinn wouldn't take being snowballed easily. I knew he'd revise plans and adjust the day-to-day activities. I subconsciously did the same thing.

When my friends left, they took Raegan with them. I went to Quinn's place. This would be temporary, or we would move from house to house to avoid staying in one place as a group. Knowing Quinn and my friends would be around all the time wouldn't be so bad. We didn't have a choice. Everything changed again. Crucial decisions on my part needed to be made soon in order to benefit everyone.

"Where did you and Garrett go?" I asked Quinn when we were finally alone.

"For starters, we went to look at a car I picked out sometime back. I had decided against it until now. I'm picking it up tomorrow."

"I can only imagine," I mumbled.

"You know I'm not really upset about my car being smashed. It's the message that bothers me."

"Yeah, that was very loud and clear. What else did you do?"

Quinn hesitated. "We went to see your parents."

"Why didn't you tell me?"

"I didn't mean to go behind your back. I thought it'd be easier coming from me instead of you. I thought you'd downplay it, which would make them worry more. So, I was very straightforward with your parents about everything and told them we were teaming up. Nobody gets left alone."

"And Mom didn't fight you on this?"

"You have to remember, your parents and I have more history and recollection of dealing with unwanted nuisances. You may have known them longer, but your memory loss sets you apart," Quinn explained, yawning and turning over to face the ceiling.

My complete and utter lack of key knowledge that could help us all remained trapped in a time warp I couldn't seem to retrieve. I'd become the weak link.

"Don't think twice about it. You can't help it. Your birth parents did what they could to save you, and in the end, made you stronger. So don't go twisting that overactive mind of yours and feeling guilty about what you can't contribute." Quinn turned over and looked seriously into my eyes. "Just keep yourself alive and out of trouble."

It seemed like a very long night. I tossed and turned and woke up several times because I thought I heard a rustling sound or something moving in the distance. The wind howled, a neighborhood car pulled up, and even a dog barked once or twice. Quinn and Garrett had set up defenses around the duplex short of an advanced security system. I'm sure my other friends had done the same thing. Oscar stayed with Raegan. His keen senses would alert them when trouble approached. He was just that type of watchdog.

*

For the next few days, my friends and I continued to live our version of normal, which included school, work, and spending time at the hidden loft. The significant difference, no one wandered off alone. We couldn't take any chances; we also varied our routes. Stipulations had been agreed upon and enforced for our safety. Besides an increased vigilance, nobody wanted to feel defeated.

"How's Noelle feeling about all of this? I mean, she's our friend, so doesn't she feel a bit left out that you asked her not to come around here?" Raegan asked me as we took a different route to class.

"It's only temporary. It's actually a good thing she doesn't go to school here. The last thing I'd want is another friend of mine being a target of some vindictive group. She understood. She's being careful, and she's keeping friends nearby. She'll let us know if something's wrong. I don't want whoever's after us to know she's a close friend."

Raegan agreed.

"It's you that I'm more concerned about. You've been thrown in with us, and you won't be able to defend yourself if anything happens. You can back out anytime."

"Leave you guys? Uh-uh. You're my friends. What would I do without you? And I can't leave Alex, so don't worry about me. I'm fast on my feet, and I can move through the crowds. I know how to stay invisible," Raegan said optimistically.

"Not with that red hair of yours."

"So I'll wear a hat," Raegan said with a quick grin.

I wasn't convinced.

"Listen, class is starting. I'll wait for you here, and then we'll meet up with Quinn," she said before making a quick turn and walking into the room.

My class was just across the street and students remained everywhere. In two minutes, I would be seated in my chair. Quinn knew where I'd be today if we didn't show up to meet him afterwards. Of course, Raegan and I planned to take a different route to a café that none of us has ever been to. No routines.

The students scurried into the lecture hall. I looked up at the clock, noting that I had five minutes before the session started. Something distracted me from making my way to the classroom. To my left and down the hallway, I spotted a man in the distance. He paused for a moment and then turned away when he realized he'd drawn my attention. He moved down the hallway, turned to the right, then disappeared from sight. Even though I knew better, I followed him. I needed to find him. I reached the same hallway he'd taken, but no one lingered.

Where are you? I wondered.

My options pointed to the right again, which would lead me into the open atrium at the center of the building. If I went to the left, I would wind up outside. I went with my gut instincts and headed outside.

No familiar faces nearby. Most of the students were now inside. I made my way farther into the grounds to search for the stranger. Nothing. Then, I noticed the mystery man lingering near a cluster of buildings. My body transported ahead. The stranger turned around, surprised to find himself face to face with me. We stared at each other for a moment, eyes never shifting and mutually curious. I felt his fear as he froze in front of me. He turned away and began to move again.

"Nathan, wait," I called out to him.

He stopped, but kept his back to me. Then, he darted into a shaded section of the pathway. I hurried to catch up to the man I eagerly wanted to know again.

"Nathan, *please.*"

He halted in the middle of the greenery, his back to me. "I knew you'd follow."

"I just want to talk to you."

He turned around. His defenses seemed to disappear, his mature and warm face no longer hidden. Nathan extended his shaking hands. "I'm sorry for being so hasty. I didn't know what to expect. It's good to see you again. I'm glad you're well."

I sighed. "You don't know how happy I am to see you. Why didn't you find me after your first contact with me at the store?"

Nathan chuckled. "It was too soon. There were so many things to consider. I knew you weren't . . . the same. When did you know?"

"Not right away. Actually, not until you called the house. When I heard your voice on the phone, I finally made the connection and realized you were the same person from the store. When we went to Connecticut this last time, I knew it was you from the past even though I never saw your face."

"From the past? I see. Your trip was eventful?"

"It was eye opening. I was able to go back in time through a spell. I only heard your voice then. That's when I realized you were Nathan. And then the photo. I saw a younger version of you at the old house."

"That's remarkable. It seems so long ago."

I looked at this cautious man. "I have so many questions to ask you. How long have you been here? What do you know about what's going on? You were the first to warn me. What can you tell me about my parents?" My thoughts spilled out of me in a rush. I wanted to know everything from this man who had been a part of my family and my past.

"We haven't much time. It's not safe for us to meet, and definitely not for long," Nathan quickly said to me and took a step back.

"What's happening? You have to tell me. Please don't go yet," I begged. "We have to find a way to meet. Quinn will want to see you. My parents, the Reeds, will want to see you."

Nathan halted. He looked at me sincerely. "I've wanted to see them for quite some time, but didn't want to risk it. The Reeds are good people, like your birth parents. And Quinn, nothing would've stopped him from reaching you. That's how I got here. That's how Clara and I left New Haven."

"You were able to get away," I said, feeling relieved they had escaped the former New Haven. "Quinn would want to know. You have to meet with us. Tomorrow morning. I know of a place. There's so much we have to talk about." My curiosity and excitement soared as I spoke to the only person who'd experienced daily contact with my birth parents.

Nathan hesitated. "I don't know. We must be careful."

"I promise. We'll take the precautions. It's important that we see you and get to know you again. Maybe this last time if that's what you want. Your choice. There are things I need to know."

"If you think it'll help. All right, tell me where and when."

I quickly wrote down the information and gave him a time. "And Clara?"

Nathan became quiet. "I must go." Before I could say anything else, he spun around and swiftly departed.

"Thank you," I whispered into the wind.

I texted Quinn to tell him we'd take Raegan to Alex's place so that we could deal with other matters. He replied with three question marks, to which I responded with a single word. *Later.*

Raegan met me outside of class. "How was it?" she asked me.

"I didn't go. Something else caught my attention."

Her olive eyes grew vivid. "What happened?"

"Something good. I'll fill you in after I know more. I caught up with Nathan, and we're meeting him tomorrow."

"You mean the one from out east, who lived at your parents' place? He's here? How?" she asked me, surprised that I mentioned his name. We jumped into a cab to meet Quinn at the café. We asked the driver to drop us off a few blocks from the place.

11

BEAR WITNESS

"He's here," I said to Quinn. I paced the loft all morning. The answers were moments away, Nathan at the center of the knowledge tree. I would finally find some form of closure.

"Don't get too excited yet. We don't know what he knows."

Quinn and I decided to arrive early at the loft. We talked about traveling through the mist. He remembered seeing Nathan and Clara trail behind, but didn't realize they had entered the same stream. His travels sped by in a blur. After his voyage concluded, things moved quickly for him. He'd lived alone in modern day New Haven.

A brisk knock sounded at the door.

"You found it. It's a little tricky." I opened the door and let the stranger clad in khaki fishing hat and tinted glasses into the secret loft. His silver highlights peeked through the edges.

"It's quite a hidden place you've managed to acquire. From the looks of it, I'm certain you've spent some time remodeling," Nathan said. He scanned the entire loft from the openness of the first floor to the balcony on the second floor. His eyes widened as he spotted the weapons cabinet. "Blood sport if all else fails?"

I laughed nervously. "My friends thought it appropriate to ready ourselves in metaphysical and physical ways."

Nathan eyed the ropes and the punching bag suspended from the ceiling. Then, his attention turned to the industrial looking kitchen. "Very modern. Quite impressive."

Quinn appeared out of the shadows. "Nathan, it's been a long time."

"My God, Quinn. It's so good to see you again." The two men embraced like long lost friends.

"Knowing that you made it out of New Haven and stand before us, well, it's great news. Thank you for being courageous enough to make yourself known," Quinn praised.

"I . . . well, wanted to do it sooner, but the circumstances weren't so obvious. You understand," Nathan responded, his voice shaking.

"Say no more. We don't want to put you in any jeopardy. We're grateful that you decided to come here. We have so much to catch up on, and Eden, now Lauren, could use a refresher. Come in, and please make yourself at home," Quinn encouraged the man.

"Yes, I understand it's Lauren now," Nathan said. He hesitated at first, then took small steps inside the loft before making himself comfortable on the couch while I quickly brought him something cold to drink.

"This is nice. All of us here, together, in the present day." Nathan took a few sips of his beverage. "I have to say, watching Lauren from a distance was rather tricky. I couldn't risk getting too close. I wanted to avoid being recognized by you, by her, and her family, even though I've aged."

"I can still see your face. It's still you," Quinn responded sincerely. "I'm actually glad you didn't come forward and risk being known. We've had some run-ins with Mercedes and Nicholas, and I'm sure they have other people working with them—wizard and human alike. We just don't know who."

"Yes, I'm aware of their presence. They managed to come through, Raefield's accomplices," Nathan said, frowning.

I took in a small breath. "And what about Clara?"

Nathan shook his head. He averted his eyes. "I lost her. She wasn't there when I came out. I don't know what happened. She was in my reach one moment, and then she was gone."

"I'm so sorry she's not with you. I know how important she is to you. Whatever we can do for you, please let us know," I said to him as I reached for his hand. He no longer felt like a stranger. I looked over at Quinn.

"Yes, I hope that my wife has found a place in time in which she can fend for herself. I know she's a strong woman, but we are out of place, and the thought of her traveling alone saddens me," Nathan said, his face grim.

"We'll do everything we can to find her," Quinn offered, consoling the man.

I remembered people telling me Clara's impact and value in my life when I had lived in New Haven. They had left their home to escape Raefield and to help us. Yet, I couldn't feel as hopeful as Quinn that we could find her. My thoughts moved to the sacrifices they had made for us, especially for me. The knot in my stomach returned.

"Nathan, you've done so much for me, and you've given up so much. I don't know how to make it up to you for everything," I said to him.

"I don't want you to feel responsible. We had to leave. It wasn't safe for us anymore once everything came out in the open. Once your parents were gone." Nathan looked at me with sympathetic eyes. "Raefield would have tortured us because we knew your family, or he'd have simply killed us. We couldn't stay. We needed to go when Quinn left, or we would have found ourselves in great pearl," he explained to me. "Tell me, what is it you want to know that would help you?"

I reached into my bag. "This. You and Clara must've hidden these items knowing I would find it. What does this mean?" I gave him the manila envelope.

Nathan looked at all the photos and he read the poem. He scrutinized the encrypted word. He looked unmoved. "I assumed you knew, because you were the one who gave these items to us before your struggle with Raefield and his men, and before you departed through the mist. You asked us to keep the contents inside this envelope safe, just in case something happened to you. And we did, in the secret place, which we showed you. It was afterwards, in the present day, when I realized you weren't yourself and that you might not have found it. That was when I decided to approach you at the store."

"So, I never said anything to you about the photos or the people standing behind my parents or these messages?"

"I'm sorry, dear. We never understood their significance, but we obviously saw that they were important to you," he said, his tone consoling. "And I gather you never mentioned them to the Reeds or to Quinn."

I shook my head.

"I'm sure she had good reason," Quinn said. "It must've been important enough that her birth parents entrusted her with something significant. Perhaps out of fear that if too many people became involved, things could accidentally fall into the wrong hands. She's not so different from the Eden we once knew."

"That, I would agree. Your parents had the utmost faith and trust in you. Dear Phillip and Faye," Nathan said, sighing.

"To their demise, it seems," I said.

"Hush. Don't say those things. You did everything you could. You would've been lost, too, had you gotten closer. And what would that have gained? No, Lauren, your survival is a testament to your parents' legacy. You carry their strength in you, combined with your own. By escaping, you kept a greater power out of Raefield's hands. Your parents knew that much," Nathan said emphatically.

I couldn't argue with him. I lacked any reason to go against the man whom my parents had trusted. Yet, a part of me believed a connection existed between the hidden treasures and the man who stood before us.

"There's something else Lauren and I have been wondering," Quinn began. "The house fire . . . was it you?"

Nathan became quiet. An uneasy expression etched his face. "We did what we thought was the right thing to do at the time. There were so many questions, and so many inquiries. People knew very little about Eden at the time, since she hadn't lived in New Haven for long. Her parents wanted it that way, so it became easier to erase her existence. She could quietly disappear into history, like a niece they'd cared for who suddenly returned home. Nobody would think twice."

"And the bodies?" I asked him.

"The poor souls. They were unknowns, already deceased.

It was a delicate matter, but a necessity to change the outcome. Of course, a handful of your kind knew what really happened. I was able to persuade a few of them to bring in the bodies. The ones who remained feared retaliation by Raefield and his men for sympathizing with your family, or if suspicion arose of Raefield's possible involvement in your family's demise. They kept quiet. The Reeds and Dr. Sendal had already left with you, and Quinn was determined to find you."

"In an attempt to soften the blow," I muttered. "The general public had no idea, and the rest that knew were either gone or too afraid."

Nathan nodded. "We didn't know if any of you would come back. We didn't know how long we would stay in New Haven. Once you, your parents, and the Reeds were gone, disorder followed within the coven."

"You did the right thing. It was a dangerous time," Quinn reassured him.

Nathan fidgeted. I touched his arm. "When did you get my parents' charms?"

He stopped moving. "Your father . . . a few days before their deaths, he instructed me to take their gifts if anything happened to them, and to keep them safe for you. We were able to retrieve them and put them with the rest of your belongings."

"They knew something might happen to them," I said. I felt sick inside. "I knew something might happen to all of us." Just like my parents, I had given Nathan and Clara personal items for safekeeping.

Nathan scrambled for his belongings. He looked weary and tense. "I've stayed too long. I must go."

I reached for him again, but he'd already put on his hat and shades. "What can we do to help you? You shouldn't be alone."

"I'll be fine."

Quinn quickly slipped something into Nathan's coat pocket as he tried to leave. "Please, take this. If we could do more, we would."

"I couldn't. You'll need this," Nathan replied, taking out the folded money.

"We have enough. It's nothing compared to everything you've done," Quinn replied.

"Thank you. It's . . . challenging being out here in the new world." Nathan zipped up his jacket. "It's wonderful to see you again, but we can't meet anymore. They'll find us. Please be careful."

"Nathan . . . you can stay with us," I pleaded.

He walked out the door and into the open. I felt the cold autumn air push against my face. With a loud thud, the heavy door of the loft closed us in again. Nathan had come into our lives like a warm, turbulent breeze from the past, only to quickly leave us with still unanswered questions.

"Do you think we'll see him again?" I asked Quinn.

"I think he'll find us when he's ready."

*

I still had Nathan's visit fresh in my memory even a week later. He'd reappeared in my life, only to suddenly vanish as if he'd never existed. I didn't feel him close by anymore, although I constantly looked for him and wondered where he'd gone. Quinn understood my quest to find him again and to help him search for his wife. We owed him that much. I owed him everything.

I dropped Raegan off at her class and met Elsie and Justin for art history.

"Did you hear what happened?" asked a student walking briskly away.

I looked ahead. A small crowd had formed in the distance, and it continued to grow larger. The paramedics, a fire truck, and the police arrived in the area around the performing arts center. They rushed into the music hall. Several students behind me sprinted past me. I sped up. My heart managed a few agonizing beats and raced ahead.

A student said on his cell phone, "Yeah, I heard it was one of the professors. They found his body in a practice room."

I darted ahead. In no time, I maneuvered through the crowd and into the heart of the commotion.

"Please, everyone, make some room for the medical crew," the department chair called out.

I slipped into the familiar practice room. Broken violins, scattered music sheets, cracked bows, and tossed chairs had turned this harmonious room upside down. The acoustic padded walls and ivory piano keys no longer appeared inviting. It wasn't the disarray that caused me to make a complete stop and fill me with alarm. Splattered blood covered the tranquil room.

I gasped at the lifeless body lying on the floor.

"Huh!"

"It's just me, Lauren," Elsie said gently. She took hold of my shoulders. "He was one of yours?"

"Yes . . . Professor Sobel." My voice cracked.

"We'll know more once the autopsy is done. My guess is he's been down for less than an hour. The coroner will take over," a first responder muttered to the police officer.

"The cuts are deep to the stomach and along his neck," another medic commented. He lifted his gloved hand, covered in Professor Sobel's blood.

"Okay, everyone. Please back up and let the police do their work."

The crowd moved away. Elsie and I managed to stay close by to watch the events unfold. The tension in my face and head lit up.

They moved his lifeless body and zipped him up into a black bag, then placed him onto a gurney. In three counts, they lifted the portable stretcher from the ground up and wheeled away the once kind and effusive professor. I wanted to scream.

"I'm so sorry, Lauren," Elsie said, trying to console me.

The forensics team remained. They photographed everything in and around the gruesome scene. One of the team members used metal tweezers to carefully pick up some broken strings covered in blood. He placed them into an evidence bag. They took notes and placed markers on anything suspicious. They dusted for prints and used a special light to illuminate hidden evidence. The lead detective spoke into a recorder. I couldn't divert my focus from all of the blood in the room.

"Close off this area," the detective ordered his personnel. "Nobody goes in."

"I just heard. What happened?" Justin said, coming up behind us.

"Professor Sobel. He was murdered," Elsie said in a low voice.

Most of the spectators scattered in a frenzy, holding onto each other and weaving away from the vicious scene. "The killer could still be on campus," a student said.

"Let's get out of here," Justin said to Elsie and I.

"Wait." I watched a detective and a school administrator attempt to interview a crying girl.

". . . It was so awful. I went to see him for a lesson, and his body looked lifeless," she said in between gulps of tears. Her voice shook. "When I saw the blood . . . and he didn't move . . . I screamed. That's when some of the other students came by."

That was all I needed to hear. The three of us hurried out through a back entrance and onto the open campus. The media arrived in full force. Chaos and fear lingered around us as students scurried in disarray. Mayhem now dominated the once orderly campus.

My phone rang. "I know. We're on our way back. I'm getting Raegan."

"Was it your music instructor?" Quinn asked on the other line.

"Yes, it was Professor Sobel." My voice shook. I ended the call.

"Quinn?" Elsie asked.

I nodded. We quickly moved to the other building to find Raegan.

She waited for us outside. She stared at the other students as they vacated the building, as if an evacuation summoned the whole campus. "Oh, my gosh, Lauren. Is it true? They found him in a practice room?"

I didn't reply. I just grabbed my best friend, and we all raced for Justin's car.

"Alex said he was coming," Raegan told us.

"Tell him to stay put. We're leaving," I responded.

Justin sped around campus to avoid any crowds and the media. The short ride home was hauntingly silent. We reached my place in a matter of minutes, and I knew what waited inside.

"I've had it with all of this!" Alex exclaimed. "They're

playing with us, and they keep upping the stakes. Someone's blood is on their hands again! They're getting closer, and we still don't know who *they* are."

A chill reverberated through me. Professor Sobel had been innocent in this tragedy, his association with me costing him his life. The killers had made themselves heard. I tightened up inside to keep the rage from seeping out.

"Did you tell my parents?" I asked Quinn.

"No, but I'm sure they'll hear about it on the five o'clock news," he replied.

"Or, from the internet," Justin added. "Look, the Dean of Students has already issued a statement on the Northwestern site." We rushed over to his laptop and read the disturbing news.

"They don't want to speculate. They don't want to cause any panic. They're doing everything they can to work cooperatively with authorities to solve the sudden death of the unfortunate Professor Sobel. They're not pointing to foul play at this time," Alex grumbled in disgust. "It's homicide! It was a job well executed. They wouldn't offer psychologists and support personnel if they didn't think something beyond natural causes was involved."

"Alex, I'm sure they want to keep everyone calm. Nobody wants to come right out and say a murderer is running around campus," Elsie explained.

"It was definitely murder, and an outside job done to make a point! Although I'm not ruling out any student involvement that might've gotten suckered in," Alex insisted.

We all turned our heads to the sound of a car pulling up the driveway. Cameron's truck.

"We would've been here sooner, but Gavin and I decided

to hang around campus and see what we could find out."

"Well, the news is spreading pretty fast. I'm sure it's going to be chaos for a while," Justin said. "Did anyone talk to Noelle?"

"She's with some friends. She heard about it. She wants to come over later," Elsie said.

I shook my head. I was fed up. "No! I can't have any more people, whom I care about, involved or be used as possible targets, because someone wants to get to me. *This needs to stop! Now!* If Mercedes and Nicholas want to confront me, then I'll deal with them myself!"

Everyone fell silent. I surprised myself with the sudden venting. Even Alex didn't know what to say.

Quinn reached out to me. "We don't know for sure if they've directed these events. We can't risk you doing that."

"But someone's setting us up, and they're trying to see what we'll do and how we'll react," I responded. "Either way, I'm sure they're associated with Mercedes and Nicholas."

"It appears that way, which is why we can't take the bait." Quinn turned to Cameron and Gavin. "What have you heard?"

"Someone said a well-dressed man was seen walking around that part of campus before Sobel was found. He thought the guy was just another professor," Cameron said. "He didn't see the man's face to get a good description."

"We also heard someone putting instruments away near the practice rooms. He had scars on his face, a shorter man. The witness said the person didn't look familiar. She thought he was a hired assistant," Gavin added.

"It could be anyone. Who knows who else is working with them? There's no running now. They're just toying with us until the moment they spring their big surprise." Alex pounded his fist on the table. "I'm getting myself ready for this shakedown!"

"Alex, man, don't do anything crazy," Gavin cautioned.

"Crazy? That's subjective. Try using what we're born to do. What else is having powers if not to harness them when necessary?" Alex picked up his backpack and stomped toward the stairs. Raegan followed closely behind. "Relax, I'm not going to do anything tonight," he called over his shoulder.

"Just let him cool down. He may be hot tempered at times, but he's not stupid," Justin defended.

Quinn's stare bored through me. I avoided making eye contact, but I couldn't help envisioning a near future in which my friends and family became divided. I saw chaos, and I saw their lives uprooted. Fighting ensued and attacks came from all sides. I envisioned more death.

*

We stood at a small, remote cemetery in Evanston on a crisp Fall day to listen to the eulogy for Professor Sobel. He would've wanted it this way. Faculty members and students from the music department and around campus attended his service. Everyone was still in shock or grieving deeply. Sitting across from them, I watched behind dark shades how his family and children mourned him. I felt anger and self-loathing as I thought about the brutal attack that resulted in his death. All I wanted was revenge. Quinn, Garrett, Raegan, and Elsie accompanied me to the funeral service for support. My parents attended, because they knew the professor. Their watchful eyes conveyed their heightened alertness to any unexpected events that might occur during his funeral.

"The police still have no leads on his case. All of the

evidence points to murder, which we already knew, but there are no suspects and we don't even have video surveillance of anything unusual. The Brandts and the Fozis have kept a watchful eye on Mercedes and Nicholas. They were nowhere near the professor when this took place, but it doesn't mean they weren't involved somehow," Dad informed all of us as we walked away from the gravesite. "How're you holding up, Lauren?"

"As best as I can. I just feel terrible for his family," I said and turned around to see them place flowers on his grave. "I wish I could've done something to prevent this."

"There wasn't anything you could do, honey. It's a terrible loss, but you can't protect everyone. The attackers knew that. Neither Mercedes nor Nicholas has accepted any responsibility. They've denied any direct involvement, but we're not convinced they didn't know who ordered the attack," Mom said, trying to console me. "If anything happens to you. . . ."

"I'm on that one, Helen," Quinn chimed in.

Mom nodded.

I faced her before getting into the car. "No, I won't allow them to intimidate me or to go after the people in my life just so they can throw it in my face. They can't do that and not expect me to react."

"I know it's hard for you to sit back and do nothing. But please, don't go looking for them. It might be what they want. We don't know who all is involved," Mom warned me. She gave Quinn a stern look. "Give us time to sort this out."

I nodded, then hugged my parents as if I might do something they'd disapprove. They climbed into their car. I watched their black car travel along the narrow road, moving as far away from me as possible.

12

FRAGMENTS, LINES, AND FISSURES

The mood on campus improved slightly even if the police and my parents still had no leads. Whoever had attacked Professor Sobel disappeared as easily and as quietly as he'd appeared. We remained vigilant.

I subconsciously passed the music room several times to feel out the last moments leading up to the attack. If being a witch meant I possessed any clairvoyant powers, then testing them out could only help. What was the point of being different if one couldn't use every power source?

I moved closer to the yellow tape spread across the double doors. My hands traced the plastic edges of the warning sign until my palms pressed against the door. Life and death crossed paths. I took a deep breath, focusing my energy on the room in front of me. The stillness inside the room echoed a deathly calmness that sent a chill through me. I knew this room, and I knew how sound could be minimized within the padded walls of this closed chamber. The struggle would've been muted.

My fingers ran across something dried along the door

panel. I looked at the maroon spot. A missing piece left behind. By natural instincts, I placed my palm over his blood. The rush came strong and fast.

The images appeared hazy and fragmented, then clarity surfaced. The professor sat alone in the room to review some music while he waited for a student. The image changed. A man entered the room. I couldn't see his face. He had straight, shoulder length, brown hair, and he wore a nice suit. They talked pleasantly for a time, like colleagues. Then, a struggle took place. The suited man covered Professor Sobel's mouth with his hand. He writhed and gasped, then he fell into a deep sleep. That man's hand changed from elegant to rough with long nails. Another man entered the room. His face appeared distorted. I saw hair-covered, boney hands and a ring of gold on the third finger. A symbol had been engraved on the ring. The second man held up the limp Professor Sobel, while the man in the suit reached inside his suit pocket and pulled out a long, shiny blade. With the thrust of his hand, the stranger made a clean midline incision across the professor's stomach. Blood and fluid spilled out of the cavity. My body shook from the images I witnessed. I stopped the search. I wanted to run inside and save the professor, but I knew I couldn't.

I pushed forward for the truth, resuming my search. The well-dressed man pointed to the right side of Professor Sobel's neck. Another cut was made, this time even quicker. Additional fluid poured out. The man took the knife and flung the professor's blood across various points of the room. I bit back my screams and my desire to rip apart the culprit. I couldn't stop now; this would be the only way to save him. I pressed my hand against the panel once more. A third and final cut was delivered into the victim's leg, deep and intentional. The shorter man dropped the professor's body to the ground. I reached out to the fallen man in my vision.

A hand touched my shoulder. I jumped.

"Alex, I didn't hear you coming." I released the memory. The maroon fragment broke apart and dispersed into the air.

"That's the problem with you stone heads. It's all euphoric and cerebral until someone sneaks up on you."

My breathing sounded labored. "You scared me. I'm not that bad."

"Oh, yeah, then why didn't you know I was here?"

"I was concentrating."

"Seems more like breaking into an *Off Limits* zone. Find anything good?"

"Definitely murder."

"What did you see, Lauren?" Alex's eyes narrowed.

I recapped everything my power of vision had permitted me to see. I left out no details. We needed all sources and angles to find the killers before they struck again. Before a war broke out.

Alex's eyes widened. He looked over his shoulder and scanned the area around us, and then turned back to the door. "Why aren't you with the others? Shouldn't you be on some form of lockdown?"

"Shouldn't you?"

"I'm on my way to get Raegan. What's your excuse?"

"Someone needs to find some answers."

"Maybe they're more obvious than you think."

My concentration broke. I couldn't study the room with Alex hovering over me and disrupting my mood. "Since you seem to know so much, why don't you share your wisdom with me?"

"I think you've found something. I think the spirits are trying to tell you who the killer is, perhaps someone you already know."

I remained silent. Had the other side attempted to reach out to me?

"He was murdered. That, we know. Are you sure you don't know who the person is?"

I shook my head. I looked at the spot on the panel where the evidence had lurked, now lost and floating as dust. Professor Sobel's murderer remained at large.

Alex chuckled. "Let's go. Best to stay in groups."

The answers behind closed doors remained unsolved. Only Professor Sobel knew what had happened. And the killers, but only one party could corroborate if forced to confess. A challenge I would take.

"Are you coming?" Alex asked impatiently.

"Sure."

As I trailed after Alex, a strong pull from the door called out to me, begged me to return. More answers or more riddles? I couldn't decide. I sensed danger, too. My heart raced erratically.

"What's wrong?" Alex asked.

"Something's there, I think. I mean, it's nothing . . . nothing at all."

"Then let's go."

*

We all huddled in our small groups and waited for the inevitable to happen. Had fear disabled us from life, or were the events hyped up because they had gotten to us? We still remained targets. That truth was a constant. At times, I found myself conflicted with my feelings.

"What's wrong with you, Oscar?" Raegan demanded of the beagle. The other animals in the house stirred, as well.

"It's just Gavin and Cam," I said to the dog.

"He's been so jumpy lately. Guess he's feeding off of everyone else's tension vibes."

"Hey, Lauren . . . Raegan. We'll try not to make a mess," Gavin promised. "It's only for a few days, then we'll switch off until this thing blows over."

"I know it's not what you wanted to do, but staying together seems the only way. Even Chelsea is staying at my parents' place after Mom pleaded with her."

"Everyone seems to be on code yellow, waiting for the final call," Gavin added.

I helped them put their stuff in the living room. Raegan planned to stay at Alex's place, and I would go next door. Oscar barked again when someone knocked at the door.

"The party has arrived. We bear gifts, and enough food for everyone," Alex said in a cheerful manner. "Isn't this fun, all camped out together like in the olden days?"

"Who's old? It seems like yesterday we hiked in the woods and set up tents. Now, it's survival parties and sleepovers for everyone," Justin responded in an annoyed tone.

"I don't mind camping out. What else are we going to do?" Elsie said, shrugging her shoulders.

"That's the attitude. When everything starts to go downhill, and you're waiting for the next attack, why not have a party?" Alex replied, still in a good mood.

"Just put the food in the kitchen and make yourselves at home," I said, rolling my eyes.

"And we shall," Alex responded.

"*Arf, arf! Grrr.*"

"Stop it, Oscar! You're really on a roll today," Raegan

scolded him. She looked through the door hole. "It's Quinn and Garrett. Nobody scary." She opened the door.

"Man, I can feel the energy in this place a mile away," Garrett said to everyone as he walked through the door. "Are you sure this was a good idea? Anyone with half the brain power can find his way here."

"I'm sure they know this neighborhood and who lives here. It's the company that's superior," Alex said from the kitchen. He set up two plates. The rest of my friends piled on their food.

Oscar ran up to Quinn, but instead of growling at him, he heeled.

"Guess you're his new best friend. You got him to calm down," Raegan said.

"He's good like that," I said to Raegan.

"Dogs are keen. They know what's going on. Little Oscar can pick up everything." Quinn reached down for the dog. "Lauren, maybe you can try to read what's bothering him."

"I wish I knew dog language."

"Better get your share before it's all gone. Can't be caught running out of gas," Alex said to Quinn and Garrett.

"We already ate. I'll replenish before night," Quinn said to him.

I consumed my food in no time. I agreed, the best advantage would be to keep our strength up.

"Lauren, can I see the pictures you got from your parents?" Cameron asked.

I looked over at Alex and Raegan. Alex shrugged. "It doesn't hurt to get a second opinion."

I reached into my bag and pulled them out, along with the poem and the cryptic message. "Here, maybe a fresh set of eyes can make something out of this stuff."

Cameron's analytical mind went to work. He scanned every inch of the photos and read and reread the poem and the message. He looked up at me behind skeptical eyes.

"Obviously, the words you've decoded seem to be the most important in its origin. It's clear that your parents instructed you to destroy something vital, and only you should be the one to do it. What it means, only Eden could interpret. Maybe in time that'll be revealed."

"I guessed that much, except for the part where only *it* could be destroyed by me. That makes sense if I have to be the bearer. The secret message was for me," I said.

"After Alex told me it was a von Eichendorff poem, I did some research. He was known for his romantic prose and deep sense of nature in his writings and poems. What he was also known for was fairytale like stories. The title has been translated into *Moonlit Night* or *Night of the Moon*, so there are also variations in the body of the poem. But your version shouldn't be completely off from the original meaning."

"Okay, we got that much after dissecting it. What are you trying to say, Cameron?" Quinn asked, fully tuning into Cameron's theories.

"It's very mystical and magical, but it seems to represent a real place. It's a place of open land or woods with flowers and all the pleasantries, and the air sweet and fresh like a nature preserve or a peaceful retreat."

"Or a garden," I whispered and turned to face Quinn. He stared at me with the same skepticism and with a careful understanding of what Cameron had said.

"Yeah, something like that," Cameron continued. "I think it could be a place you've been to." He suddenly stopped talking and looked up at me. "I guess you've been there before."

Quinn remained solemn. "What else did you pick up?"

"You know, I keep looking at these photos and nothing comes up. I mean, they seem to be saved for sentimental reasons. Guess you didn't want to lose everything," Cameron replied.

"Whatever I thought at the time is a mystery to me, but I know I held on to these photos for more than sentimental reasons."

"This one; it's out of place," Cameron said, pointing to the photograph with Raefield and the two strangers. "It doesn't match your collection."

"That's the one that bothers me. Why would I keep that one if it weren't important? It has to be the two people that I don't recognize."

"I'll bet our friend Raefield would know," Alex said sarcastically.

Raegan shot him a dirty look.

"What's with the left corner? Are those markings of some kind?" Cameron asked.

"We're not sure, Cam. We don't know if, when Mom had it retouched, something got permanently etched in the corner."

"No, something else." He reached into his sack and pulled out a small spray bottle and something round. "When I work on photography, I use a little of this to illuminate a photo that's dated. It works to dissolve particles, too." Cameron carefully sprayed a small amount of fluid onto the photo. Then, he waited for it to air dry. He lifted the image up to light. "I see something."

I inched closer.

Cameron took out the eyepiece and examined the photo like a scientist would study a specimen under a microscope—every angle, every dimension, and with magnification to see what the naked eye couldn't see. "It's the next best thing to a microscope, and much lighter. Here, the fluid brought out the spot that was hidden. It resembles the same lines as these under the thicker markings." He handed me the picture to examine.

"Wow, that really worked well— Ouch!"

Cameron pulled a piece of my hair between his fingertips and examined it under his eyepiece. After a moment, he took the photo right out of my hands. He went back and forth between the photo and the strand of my hair. He then placed them side-by-side. "If I didn't know any better, it looks like a few hairs got caught in the photo. Minus the DNA proof, I think they could be yours."

Everyone in the room turned to look at me.

"Wait a minute. Are you saying those are Lauren's hair strands? That would mean she was there," Alex exclaimed, his brown eyes going wide.

"I don't want to jump to conclusions, but I'm betting they belong to her. Here, Lauren, look for yourself." Cameron handed me the items.

I looked at the photo and the strands in the corner of the image and then at my own hair. Under the lens, the markings in the photo resembled hair strands. I became speechless. I handed the picture and lens to Quinn.

"A regular scope would define it more, but I'm certain that's hair," Cameron said confidently. His tone changed when he looked at me again. "I think getting your memory back would be the best thing."

Quinn moved closer and put his arm around me.

I let out a heavy sigh. "It seems like the answers are right in front of me, but they keep moving beyond my grasp."

"It's not your fault," he reassured me.

"Um, is there anything else of value?" Cameron asked.

I reached into my bag. "The only things I have left are my parents' charms. Who knows what further significance and value they have."

"Well, we know what it's suppose to do. I wonder if it's able to go beyond the usual cloaking function." He returned the necklace to me. "And your father's?"

I gave Cameron the coin. "That's odd. It's not something you'd wear. He'd always need pockets to keep it with him. Strange." Cameron continued to examine the coin, flipping it over and over. The green center shimmered every time he turned the coin.

"What is it?" I asked him.

"I was thinking, in mythology, coins or flat metal objects were useful beyond monetary value. They acted as keys. They fitted into compartments or slivers that were precisely programmed to release once a coin was inserted," Cameron said.

"A key?"

"It was just a thought."

"No, you could be right. I never thought of it like that, but it makes sense. For all I know, it might as well be a key. Wonder what it opens?"

"Guess you'll have to find out," Cameron replied.

Alex abruptly stood. "I think we've had enough legends and tales for one night. I'm beat. Let's all get some sleep and revisit this in the morning."

"I couldn't agree with you more this time," Elsie replied, yawning as she got up from her chair. "We just seem to get bits and pieces. Wish it would just all come together and get it over with."

Elsie and Justin left for their place, followed by Alex and Raegan and a trailing Oscar, the dog now more obedient. I grabbed a few things for my trip next door.

"Hey, Cameron. I really appreciate your insight tonight. It does put another spin on the things I have."

"I don't mind. I actually find putting this mystery together interesting. Except for the poor professor."

I nodded. "You and Gavin make yourself at home. The sofa pulls out, and the floor is large enough for his blowup mattress. There's still plenty of food in the fridge."

"Don't worry, we can manage. See you tomorrow." Cameron waved to me as I closed the door to my place.

I followed Quinn to his side of the house. Garrett had returned to their place before we arrived, and he was watching football.

"Why should we have to give up everything and hide under some rock waiting for something to happen? I'm gonna do what I normally do. Screw them," he said with his eyes still fixed on the TV screen.

"Doesn't make a difference to me if you watch football or jump out of a plane. Just watch your back," Quinn replied.

"Humph."

We left Garrett to his worldly treasure and headed upstairs. "Let's go downtown tomorrow. Traffic shouldn't be too bad. The others can meet us later," Quinn suggested.

"Where are we going?"

"There's a place I want to check out. We need to get supplies. Dr. Sendal suggested we get the best ingredients. We can also stop at a pawn shop, which might have some ideas about your father's coin."

"Sounds like a good idea. We can meet the others at the loft later on," I said, climbing into bed.

"Everything will work out. It has to," Quinn mumbled.

I couldn't see his eyes, only the darkness of the night, but I felt him slowly fall into a slumber that would take him to a healing and peaceful state. My eyes grew heavy. The cool breeze from the window cracked open brought in a tingling sensation of fresh air twisted with something tight. At first, I thought my imagination had gone into overdrive. The cool air continued to circulate, then a sudden change startled me. I couldn't breathe well. A suffocating blanket of heavy air tightened around my throat. I gasped. My breath shortened until it stopped.

Sometime during the night I had fallen into a deep sleep only to awaken in the early morning. I remembered light instead of darkness surrounded by a chilling bluish breeze.

*

We packed everything we could for the day into Quinn's black Escalade, knowing we might not return for the night. Quinn had settled for something substantial over a smaller car after the parking lot incident, although he had been hinting at something with mileage longevity just in case we needed to take a cross-country trip. Unfortunately, there weren't too many options at this time.

"Do you think the others will stay at the loft or go to a hotel?" I asked.

"They're probably playing it by ear."

"I mean, it's not like we're running all the time, just changing things around. Don't you think?"

Quinn remained silent. He continued to pack the rest of our bags and threw some extra blankets into the back seat, securing the camping gear and stocking bottles of water in the back. "We should get going."

We drove along some residential streets that we normally wouldn't take and decided not to connect onto the freeway until further south.

"Whatever happens in the next couple of days, promise me you'll keep going," Quinn said.

"You're really scaring me. Is something going to happen to you?"

"I'm being realistic. Anything could happen to any of us at anytime. I just want to make sure you get as far away and go as fast as you can if we get split up."

I stared at him harder, my eyes wide and my jaw sagging with shock. *"You think I would leave you stranded if something happens!"* I yelled at him.

Quinn looked startled, but he managed to stay focused on the road. "No, that's just it," he looked at me briefly with his piercing, gray eyes. "You'd do everything you could to save me. You'd fight, and you'd try to take anyone out. But I don't want you to do that. I want you to get away. I want you to do what it takes to survive."

My tears slowly seeped down my face, but I clenched my teeth and fought to keep my emotions in check. I hardened myself.

"Lauren, I mean it."

"Quinn," I whispered.

"If you love me, then you'll do as I ask. I'm not saying you should take off and leave your family and friends this instant. But if I don't make it, your survival has to be your priority. If they get you, we all lose."

I shook my head. Heat flushed my face. "No, you can't ask that of me. I won't run like some scaredy-cat. I won't let anyone come near the people I care about, especially you. I won't let anybody get hurt!"

"Why do you have to be so stubborn?" Quinn snapped. He shot me an angry look, but I saw pain instead of anger in his clouded facial expression. He quickly turned away to look at the open freeway ahead. He let out a heavy sigh.

"I'm not trying to fight you on this," I said calmly. "There has to be another way."

Quinn didn't say anything.

"Because I love you that much, there has to be a better way."

Quinn reached for my hand. I held his tight. His hand felt warm and familiar. I knew his touch. The blood and the electricity flowed through him and into me in this parallel circuit. It would keep us going. It would keep us strong. I would keep us alive.

"What was that?" I suddenly asked. A rush of pain traveled to my head.

"I didn't hear anything," Quinn replied. He continued to drive along the freeway when we saw the exit sign for Chinatown.

"That." The rumbling moved steadier this time. It lasted about ten seconds and shook the heavy car before coming to a complete stop. "What's going on?"

Quinn veered off the highway at the next exit, and made a sharp right turn onto the first street. He stopped the car next to the curb. "I don't know. Turn on the radio."

I flipped on the radio and scanned the stations for any available newsfeed.

"This is Adam with WGKO. Whoa, did you feel it? Yes, folks, we at your source for the latest have reported seismic activity here in Chicago land. That's right, everyone, an earthquake here in Chicago. We're confirming it with the USGS. This is big, folks! Hold on tight. We're getting information from IEMA to prepare us for this type of event. . . ."

"An earthquake? This isn't right." I rolled down the window and scanned the area.

"No, it's too right for something else." Quinn studied the buildings ahead. We'd ventured into a warehouse division. Some buildings appeared deserted while others brimmed with activity. Trains nearby rolled along the tracks. "Change of plans. Let's go—"

The rumbling and the movement started up again. The ground shook more forcefully this time. Quinn and I jumped out of the car and stood still, unsure where to run next from the moving ground. I grabbed his hand. The tremors soon stopped when my phone rang.

"Mom, I can barely hear you. There's a lot of static . . . No, we're okay . . . What did you say? You're breaking up again."

Quinn studied the area around us.

"Mom, can you hear me? We're . . . Yes, I think we can."

"What did she say?"

At this time, the city emergency sirens sounded, loud enough to deafen. They normally went off before a tornado or other predicted severe weather patterns. In this case, an earthquake would be unexpected.

We got back into the SUV. "She wants us to meet them. She said they've been trying to call me even before the tremors began, because something felt out of place. The signal went down. Even her landline didn't go through."

"Buckle up. It may be a bumpy ride."

I checked my phone again, finding messages from my friends that now only appeared.

"I don't like this," I muttered.

"We're getting out of here. Now."

13

STORM CHASERS

"Quinn, say something."

He stared at the open road. His determination to get us out of town and away from the epicenter didn't waver. Would it be worse elsewhere? Quinn drove through the narrow streets and made rash turns to avoid the potholes that had formed from the brutal winter and the stormy rains this past year. I grasped the handle above my seat. Even in the Escalade, the bumps were unavoidable.

Why had this happened? I looked at the date on my phone. September 29. The harvest moon fell on this weekend.

I scanned my phone as fast as I could. "I can't find anything that says there's been recent tremors in the Midwest."

"No, I wouldn't think so," Quinn replied solemnly. He never took his eyes off the road. He pushed on the gas.

I swallowed hard. The rawness in my throat and the tightness in my neck hinted at troubles to come. I didn't want to imagine the worse.

"What are the others saying? Is there any damage by your parents' place?"

"She said there was trembling in Evanston. Alex, Raegan,

Justin, and Elsie are in the city north of us. They've seen lights go out and buildings shake. There's some street damage. They're going to try to head back home."

"Did you hear from anyone else?"

"Nothing from Cameron, but Noelle just texted to say she saw the sky go dark then a hazy white—"

Quinn slammed on the brakes.

I extended my arms and gripped the dashboard to soften the blow. I looked up, startled.

". . . A blue and white haze."

Quinn and I stared at the imposing city in front of us. The previously beautiful day, now draped in smoky clouds, rolled across the skyline like a net ready to fall.

My phone rang, but it kept losing its signal. "I can't get through!"

"Hold on."

Quinn made a sharp left turn away from the city and the backed up traffic. We couldn't move very fast. I saw people running into the streets, back and forth, unsure where to go, and people running into each other to push their way through. The streetlights weren't coordinating, which added to the traffic confusion. Office building lights flickered on and off.

Quinn finally found an opening and drove quickly out of the city.

I closed my eyes and focused on the best way I knew to get us beyond the city. The heavy car lifted off of the road and moved faster than Quinn had driven. The car climbed fifty more feet before a strong pull brought it back down to the ground.

"It seems magnetic, too," I muttered.

"Like energy is being drawn in," Quinn commented.

I looked at the erratic GPS. "It's messed up. It keeps rerouting us. I'm turning it off."

Quinn swirled again to find a shortcut through one of the side streets. *"C'mon, c'mon!* Let's move it."

"Turn that way," I said to him, pointing to a street that looked familiar. "Go right, then straight about five blocks; the ramp should be coming up. Let's hope the freeway isn't totally jammed."

Quinn roared ahead. He passed anything and anyone who stood in his way. He suddenly slowed down.

"What are you—?"

The earth began to shift again. First, a gentle vibration, then a heavier tremor, which lingered. I grabbed the door handle again. "Whoa." I looked outside of my window. The sky began to clear. The dark, thick clouds parted overhead.

"Not good," Quinn said under his breath, trying not to curse. He pressed down on the gas again once the tremors stopped, but then stopped instantly.

The ground shook more rigorously. I grabbed Quinn's arm and closed my eyes for a moment. "Is now a good time to get out of the car?"

Before Quinn could answer, I squeezed his arm tighter. I turned around from the noise echoing behind us, and I watched in horror as a building a few blocks away crashed to the ground. The rubble and the debris sifted through the air atop the collapsed pile.

"Look behind us."

Quinn looked up into the rearview mirror then sped ahead. He squeezed my hand. "Remember what I said."

I didn't want to argue. I went numb and focused on the sudden cracks in the road that crept alongside the car and appeared to move ahead of us.

"The ramp," I pointed out.

Quinn tightly gripped the wheel as he made the cloverleaf loop, burning the tires into the road. I watched as another office building crashed to the ground before smaller buildings in the same vicinity collapsed, as well. Piles of concrete, steel, and wood dropped like toys. Dust filled the air. Destruction surrounded us. I looked ahead. The north freeway still appeared stable.

"I'm surprised it's not more crowded," Quinn commented, still driving as fast as he could.

I became fixed on the sky. "It's so clear." The pounding in my head started up again. I sank back in my seat.

"Are you all right?" Quinn asked.

"I'm fine. Probably working myself up."

The earth shook again, this time with an added light show. Instead of the white flickering of lightning, a heavy, dark hue surged across the city. I rolled down the window.

"It's humid outside. The temperature reading says eighty-seven." I flipped the radio back on.

"*. . . Something's going on in Lake Michigan. Did you see the size of the waves? They're moving on shore.*"

"Is he *really* coming?" I asked Quinn.

"He can't be. It's not the way it happens. There isn't a destruction when someone arrives."

"Then what is it?"

"I don't know, Lauren. I really don't know," Quinn turned to me, his face tight and tension-filled, and fear shadowing his eyes.

"*. . . If this message is getting to you, take immediate action. Drop down to the ground and cover yourself. Stay indoors, but avoid falling objects. If you're driving, stay in your car, but avoid bridges and overpasses. Traffic on the western and the southern freeways is bumper* *to bumper. Don't go east and stay away from downtown. There's some room on the northern roads and the city side streets. Be advised to clear the streets and take shelter as soon as you can."*

My phone rang again. I put Alex on speaker.

"Where are you guys? We've been calling for the last hour. This is the first time I'm able to get through. Man, this wind is blowing things everywhere," he said.

"Getting off of the freeway onto Dempster. We're meeting my family. Meet us there."

"We're getting Noelle first, then we'll meet you there. She's stuck at a friend's place. I don't know where Cameron and Gavin are."

"Alex, once you pick up Noelle, just get out of the city. Head north. Get as far away as you can manage, and we'll try to meet you," Quinn ordered. "Let us know where you'll be."

"Lauren . . . Lauren? We're okay. I'm trying to stay calm."

"Raegan, I miss you guys. Elsie, are you okay, too?"

"I'm fine, but something in my hands doesn't feel right. I feel . . . charged."

"What the hell is going on? If he's coming, then I'm ready. Nobody blows in like a storm and decides to take over—"

"Alex? Alex?" The line went dead. I redialed his number. "It's not going through."

"We're getting closer. It's best they just leave."

"You know they won't."

"If this is an army, they might not stop at their objective." Quinn glanced at me with anguish-filled eyes. "They'll want to get their hands on any of us. We need to minimize any loss."

I swallowed hard. The thought of my friends or family being butchered by the deranged witches to gain power set off this silent rage inside of me. I tightened my fist to hold it in.

"Don't give in," Quinn gently said to me.

I propped up my ringing phone.

"Lauren, is that you?" Chelsea said over the speaker.

"We're okay. We're almost there." I wanted to hug my sister.

"No, don't come here! Get as far away as you can!"

"What? Mom said to meet her here. What's going on?"

"We were wrong. They're not coming here. You have to get away. They're—"

"Chelsea? Chelsea, can you hear me?" I picked up the phone and moved it around to try to get a clearer signal. "Chelsea, where's Mom? *What's happened to her?*"

". . . Storm isn't an arrival . . . It's pulling in . . . We got it wrong . . ."

"Chelsea, I'm losing you. What do you mean? Say it again."

The line completely died. I frantically tried to call her back, unsuccessfully. I tried to call my parents again. I still couldn't get through. "Mom is in trouble. We have to help her!"

Quinn hesitated. "I know it's your mom, but shouldn't we listen to Chelsea?"

I looked at him strangely. "Mom is in trouble. We have to do something! She went there. I know it."

"She's where?" Quinn shook his head and blinked quickly. "Right, right. There's a shorter way." He made another quick turn.

"Why would she go to the store when we planned to meet at their place? I'm sure she's there."

"Maybe your father went with her."

"Yeah, you're probably right. He wouldn't let her go to

the shop alone at a time like this. And neither would Chelsea or . . . *Quinn,* **watch out!"**

Quinn quickly veered away from the falling tree that came tumbling in our direction, but it managed to crash on top of the car, taking out the driver's side window. The car rolled twice from Quinn's abrupt movement. He tried to shield himself from the debris and to gain back control of the large vehicle. The SUV knocked down a metal fence, then skidded along the pavement and into a grassy knoll. The left side of the SUV scraped against an abandoned car. I heard a crunch as we rolled over an object before slamming into another tree. I jerked back into my seat as the air bags deployed. The tires hissed and the car shifted again onto one side.

I finally caught my breath and moved the seat back. I immediately reached for Quinn. "Are you okay?"

He didn't say anything. He was pushed up against the wheel after his airbags deployed then became deflated from a branch. Quinn appeared hazy, but then he looked up. I followed his gaze. The cumulus clouds took on a denser shape and turned a deep gray before the darkness moved away. The wind picked up speed again as the sky flickered and blue undertones formed. I recognized this formation.

"Yeah, I'm fine," he suddenly said and regained full consciousness. He pushed back his seat. Quinn tried to start the car again. "Let's get out of this thing and see what kind of damage we have."

"Quinn, the side of your head is bleeding." I handed him a wad of tissues.

He looked in the mirror. "It's only a scrape. I'll be fine." He pushed and kicked the bent door. It finally opened.

I jumped out of my seat and moved to his side of the car. "Let me help you out. Lean on me."

"Ouch! My knee." Quinn reached for his left knee. "It's swelling up." He took a few steps away from the car and almost fell. He reached for the left side of his body. He grimaced.

I helped him to the ground and examined his knee. I checked him over, but when I turned him to his side, I gasped. *"Quinn, you're bleeding!"* His right hand was covered in blood as he applied pressure to his left side. A wooden object stuck out of his ribs. I ran for the first aid kit in the SUV.

The wind grew stronger and more persistent, but I refused to allow it to stop me. I pushed it away from us until it lingered on the outside and waited to throw its weight back in. The wind felt angry and vengeful. It circled above us, pounding against the invisible protective layer I had formed.

"See, I took it out," Quinn said, showing me the blood soaked stick.

"This isn't the time to be funny. I've got to close it up before it gets infected," I said to him and took the supplies out. "I'm going to clean it and dress it. It might sting."

"Wonderful, my own personal nurse," he said with a faint smile. "I knew you had the magic . . . *Ouch, that smarts!*"

I flushed the deep wound and cleaned around the edges. I placed the instant clot bandage on and held pressure, then covered the site with an occlusive dressing. Then, I placed instant ice packs on his swollen knee.

"Here, drink some of this so you can heal more quickly," I instructed.

He gulped down the special tonic. "There, I should be healed, but it might take some time."

I looked up at the scornful sky. The wind died down and then picked up speed again. "We don't have much time left."

"We're close by. We can go on foot once I regain my strength. The car is totaled."

I looked at Quinn's injuries.

"Lauren, help me up. I want to see if there's any improvement."

I helped him up from the ground.

Quinn tried to walk, but I saw the pain in his face. I eased him back down. "You're not ready."

"I guess not," he replied.

I looked in the direction that led to the shop. "There isn't time." I turned back to him, feeling guilty. "Listen, I would never do this to you, but you're in the clear. You'll heal, but not quickly enough. I've got to see if Mom is still there and make sure she's not in trouble."

Quinn's face tightened. "I don't think it's a good idea. I don't want you to go alone."

"If she's in trouble, I have to help her. I'll come right back once I see that she's safe, then we can decide what to do next. If she's not there, at least we'll know she got out."

"Assuming she was ever there," he replied.

"I have a feeling she's there."

Quinn let out a heavy sigh. "All right, but *be* careful. This isn't my idea, okay? I'm concerned about your mother, too."

"I know. You'd come with me if you could."

"Make sure you aren't seen. Do what you have to do to get away."

I kissed him hard, but what I felt and tasted was heartache on my lips. "I'll be back soon."

"If you're not back in fifteen minutes, I'm hopping to the store."

I spun into motion until I became a blur. I flew like the wind, quickly reaching the perimeter of the store. I stopped at a maple tree next to another shop a few doors away and hid behind the building and the protective tree.

14

HELEN'S TRADE

I noticed a familiar looking tan Enclave parked near the shop.

The Brandts came with her? Why are they here, too?

I scanned the lot and the other stores near her shop, but I didn't see anyone familiar. The whole town seemed to have vanished. The wind howled and blew more forcefully in Evanston. Doors slammed open and closed. Debris flew everywhere. From where I stood, I couldn't see movement inside the store. With stealth-like moves, I inched closer to the shop, hiding behind brick walls and entryways of the other stores. I traced my metal bracelet and vanished.

I pressed my face up against the window without leaving a mark. I saw Mom and Aaron and Leslie Brandt. They appeared anxious and preoccupied. Leslie sipped her tea as she watched Aaron pace a few steps. Someone walked up to Mom—someone I didn't expect. Billie. *Billie?* They all seemed to be waiting for someone else to arrive.

I surveyed my surroundings again and scanned the store. Nothing appeared dangerous and no warnings flooded my thoughts. I glided through the front door like air and gently turned my bracelet.

"Mom?"

"*Lauren*. Why did you come here?" Her face tightened. Fear and worry reflected from her eyes. "You can't be here."

"I knew you'd be here, but why? What's going on? I could barely make out what Chelsea tried to tell me. She said not to come to the house, so I didn't. She said 'we were wrong', then the phone went dead before she could explain. I rushed here even though she told me to get away. I had to make sure you were okay."

Mom shook her head. Tears formed in her eyes. She reached out to me and hugged me tightly. She grabbed my face, and with a somber expression, she said, "My foolish daughter. I told you not to come, but I guess deep instead, I knew you'd do everything you could to find your family."

"I don't understand."

"Haven't I taught you better? Haven't I told you no matter what happens, you need to protect yourself?"

"So you've mentioned. But as a self-determined adult, you know I tend to go against the grain. You should know I can't leave my family if there's trouble. Besides, it sounds like Raefield isn't coming."

Leslie chuckled. "My dear, I think it's in your best interest not to find it. It seems to be attracted to you."

I laughed nervously.

"What'll we do, now that she's here?" Aaron asked and stepped forward. "Would this jeopardize our mission?"

Confusion overcame me. "Mom, why are you here and not at home, and why I was told to stay away?"

"I couldn't get through to you after our last conversation, so I told Chelsea if you called home, you shouldn't come back here to meet us. After that, I wasn't able to get through to her," Mom explained.

"The line broke apart. She said something was pulling in. Is this storm pulling something in?"

Mom's eyes widened. "What did she say exactly?"

"I only heard part of it. 'Storm isn't an arrival' and 'It's pulling in.' What does it mean?"

Mom's face twisted. She turned to Leslie and Aaron. "It can't be. Did Chelsea see something we didn't see? I couldn't reach her again."

"What can't be? And who are you meeting?" I asked them.

"We came as a peace offering. We came to negotiate with a liaison of Raefield," Mom said. "Lauren, you need to leave here. Now."

"*What?* I'm not leaving. Why would you do such a thing?"

"It was the only way to offer a truce between them and to ensure that Mercedes and Nicholas would back off," Mom said.

"And you believe them?"

"Do I trust them? No. Do I have much choice? Not really. They've been trained and ordered to hunt you down until they get what you possess that's buried deep inside your mind. I can't live like that. I can't have them go after you until the end of your existence. What is a mother supposed to do?"

Everything clicked so perfectly together in my head. "Mom, what did you agree?"

Mom lowered her head for a moment then looked up. "That my powers would be given to them. I would be stripped and drained of all the energy I possessed as an exchange for your survival. I'm the closest blood link. I'm the twin to your father. It's the best offer."

I shook my head at what she just told me; the sacrifice

she'd agreed to make on my behalf. The nightmare returned. "No. I *will* not have them take that away from you."

"What would you have me do? Let them come after you time and again?"

I didn't know if I felt anger or guilt. "I can take care of myself. There's always another way. Does Dad know about this?"

"No, he thinks we came here just in case you decided to look for us here. I convinced him to stay and ask Leslie and Aaron to join me."

"We couldn't let her go alone." Leslie turned to Billie. "Did he say he'd be here soon?"

A nervous Billie came forward. "He . . . he said you knew to meet him here at four o'clock. He wanted me to tell you that he'd be gravely disappointed if you didn't fulfill your bargain."

I glared at Billie. Her cropped, auburn hair appeared tousled and different. I stared at her transparent face until she could no longer look at me, which only lasted for a moment. I searched her anxious eyes and watched her lips quiver; a flush seeped into her face. Her neck tightened.

"I wonder if you're actually a natural blond. Perhaps you've visited me at the library this past summer, claiming to be a friend of mine?" I thought back to when Ethan had said a student was looking for me.

Mom and the Brandts looked confused.

"Oh, please. It wasn't my idea. I had no choice. They made me do it. They made me get closer to you," Billie cried out.

"Billie, what have you done?" Mom demanded, her fear apparent now.

Billie shook and she cried. *"I'm sorry. I'm so sorry for everything. They have my family. They made me leave my husband.*

They told me that if I said anything to you, they would hurt him. They told me all I had to do was get closer to—"

The wind kicked open the front door. Dust particles formed a wind tunnel in front of us before the fine powder settled, then the illumination came through. First, the image appeared subtle, then it became overpowering. The light blinded us with an intensity that mirrored the phantom image at the hotel in New Haven, its rays showering the store in a light show. Impatient and irritated, I began to force the rays back to the tunnel.

Then he walked through.

"Good afternoon everyone. Helen, I'm so glad you were able to make it on time. Such a storm we're having," the eloquent and handsome man said as he walked through the light.

"It's you," I muttered.

"It is I."

I carefully watched this man, feeling wary as he stepped forward. He circled me and smiled. His face appeared Raphael-like—timeless, handsome, and gracious—someone curious and pleasing, drawn to easily. I looked into his dazzling eyes and saw the darkness.

"I'm so glad we have the chance to meet again after our brief encounter. I had hoped to talk and to socialize with you longer at the fashion show, but you seemed ill at ease. Meeting again here, well, under these circumstances, it's not of my choice. How unfortunate we couldn't consort on better terms. I've always admired your voracity, Lauren, even at a distance. Or should I say, Eden?"

I trembled. "It's unfortunate to come down to this. Tell me, are you always operating at the whim of Mercedes and Nicholas, or just at the mercy of Raefield?"

The stranger laughed confidently. "You haven't lost your quick wit. I'm glad that hasn't changed. Dearest Lauren, how tempted I was to reveal myself to you that day with your friends around, but that would have ruined everything. No, I only allowed a brief encounter with you to lead up to this point."

"More like I was trying to get away, Mr. Ferrari."

Horus chuckled, looking quite satisfied.

Mom interrupted us. "We have a deal, Horus. I'm not sure what else you had in mind, but I didn't come here to give into your agreement for you to turn this arrangement into a folly. She's not to be touched."

"Tsk, tsk, Helen. Let's not be rash and biased. One can't help but entertain the idea of having so much energy within reach. Eden has been away for so long," Horus replied.

"It's Lauren. And I'm not your pet."

"Of course, my warrior princess. You're nobody's servant. You're in a class all your own with that shiny piece of stone wedged neatly inside that imaginative mind of yours. If only you could be separated from it."

"Horus, this is not what we agreed upon!" Mom insisted.

"Yes, you're correct on that, Helen. We did have an agreement, which I intend to fulfill. I've waited so long. And patiently. Such a very, very long time." Horus glided with ease across the floor, never touching the ground with his feet. His long, dark robe flowed richly on the ground like a garment fit for a king. "I've been held to his terms for so long, I can't even remember what it's like to be free," Horus continued on, his face captured in a reverie. "Soon." He turned to us. "I will leave with what I need."

I stepped in front of Mom. "Nobody gives herself up for me."

Horus smiled. His expression bore self-assuredness and amusement. He inched closer to me. "Giving in would be simpler," he hissed.

Horus vanished; he moved in and out of sight throughout the store. I heard him slither around us. His quiet laughter rang in my ear. This startled the Brandts. They watched his fading form carefully, their defenses up. Mom's cold expression never changed. Billie hid behind a bookshelf and kept her whimpering to a minimum. I didn't know if she feared us more than him.

The sky outside cleared before something else approached. Darkness encroached on the beacon of light in this unfortunate and dark hour. The moon had risen early. Its size and brightness appeared overwhelming, too large for the season, yet ripe enough for a special harvest.

"It's nearing," Horus said, as he emerged from the shadows.

I continued to watch the moon fill up along the horizon until it appeared within reach. I could almost touch it and feel its magnificent glory. I couldn't keep my eyes away from the mesmerizing body. The moon glowed as a river of deep red slowly crept along the edges.

"It's bleeding. The moon is bleeding," Billie said to everyone as she came out of hiding.

I looked closer. "That's not blood. It's changing."

"Yes, look carefully," Horus said. "It's a lovely sight."

The fluid continued to flow, and it covered every part of the moon in a shimmering, red glaze. The fluid turned and caramelized in layers around the moon. The outside world went completely dark. Then the fluid dissipated and vapors began to take over. Light emerged, but not a guiding light that brought hope. Hazy, blue vapors sprang to life. The mist thickened around the moon and grew dense in a cloud of blue. It began to reach beyond its host.

I knew what would happen next.

I turned to the mystical man. "No harm comes to any of them. That's my deal."

Horus laughed. "Spoken like a true negotiator. Of course, of course. I'd like nothing more than a smooth transition. See, this can all be done effortlessly. Everyone wins."

"Lauren, what are you doing?" Mom called out.

I swallowed hard as the tears weighed heavy in my eyes. "It's happening, anyway. I can't control it. It's opening up."

Horus inched closer. "She's a bright one, our Eden. She knows, because she can feel it. You've raised her well, Helen."

"This is not what we agreed on! You have to make this—"

The wind blew open the doors again. Familiar faces moved through the debris and into the open room. I steadied myself to strike first if forced.

"Is everything almost set?" Mercedes asked as she looked around the room at all the startled and horrified faces. "The moment is just right."

Mom grabbed me by the wrist and held it as tight as she could. *"She's not going anywhere."*

Horus let out a heavy sigh and put his arm around Mom's shoulder. She pushed it away. "Helen, it's been done. You can't stop it now. Everything's in motion."

"Not on false pretenses. We can stop this," Mom said with conviction.

Horus still gripped Mom's shoulder. His hand began to change.

"You. You killed him in the music room. *Why?* What did

he do to you?" I yanked my mother out of his clutches. The energy charged up in my body and waited for my command.

Steady, Lauren. One shot, and this is over.

Mom placed her arm in front of me and eased me back.

"That's correct, Helen. Guide your daughter, if necessary." Horus laughed. "Powerful. Sheer, raw energy. I can feel it. You ask why? Simple. To gather your attention. Things became too quiet. I wanted you to be alert. I needed to set things off."

I clenched my fists. *Don't let him win. This is what he wants.*

Billie, Leslie, and Aaron moved closer to Mom. Leslie drew Mom away from a potential showdown.

"What kind of people are you?" Billie asked after finding her voice.

Nicholas laughed. He seemed genuinely amused.

"Something in your worst nightmare, I'm afraid. You wouldn't understand," Mercedes replied, self-assured. "Betty, isn't it?"

"It's Billie, and try me. I've seen some pretty crazy stuff, although you guys are definitely at the top of the list."

"Well, *Billie*, you've done your part well as instructed. Now you can go," Mercedes ordered.

"You should leave, Billie. This is beyond you," Mom insisted.

"No, I'm staying. I want to see what this insanity is all about. I want to know why my family was threatened and why you need Lauren so much."

"If that's the case, then you'd better hold on to something heavy," Mercedes warned her with a devilish grin. "It's going to be electrifying."

"*Horus,* my offering is just as good," Mom pleaded.

"Helen, you are a prize all your own. But you're not Eden.

I need Eden. *He* wants Eden. I can finally be free. I can finally leave this servitude."

"No, you can't take her," Mom gasped and crouched closer to me.

Mom quickly sprang up from her bowed position, threw her arm above her head, and then back down. Leslie and Aaron followed her lead. The room shook and quivered, throwing Horus, Mercedes, and Nicholas off of their feet and hurling them to the ground. "Let's move, everyone!" Mom grabbed my hand and ran to the door, but we were met with a startling discovery at the exit.

A crowd of disfigured people pushed their way into the store. They set up a barrier, which forced down the blockade that Mom, Leslie, and Aaron erected. I had never seen these people, but I knew who they were. They had been brought here from their hiding place deep in the mountains. Forgotten witches. And now, they wanted their misguided redemption.

"Leave this place!" I called out and pushed my will against theirs. Their fragile blockade collapsed in seconds against my strength. They could never hold against me. The forgotten witches collided against the store's wall.

"Hurry!" Mom ordered everyone.

We ran for the door again when an agonizing pain ripped through me.

"Ahhh!" A magnetic force pushed me down to the ground. I clutched my head. I writhed in pain.

"Lauren!" Mom cried, reaching down to protect me.

When the pain subsided for a moment, I looked up through a window and saw the sky turn a magnificent liquid blue. It swirled like candy, rich in sweetness and full of life, ready to be shaped. The form grew and reached out to me.

Horus, Mercedes, and Nicholas approached us.

"Yes, Lauren, you know you can't do that and not know the consequences. *For every action, there is an equal and opposite reaction.* It just brings you closer to the calling," Horus reminded me.

"*Helen,* do you think your simple trick can get you out of here? There's a reason you can't leave until this is done," Mercedes pointed out and straightened her outfit as she came closer to Mom. "I'm just as strong as you are. You and your weak twin, who think they have all power over everyone. Well, that's going to change. Everything is turning over."

Nicholas looked amused again. He never flinched since his arrival.

"How much longer, Horus?" Mercedes asked.

"It's not much longer. Isn't that right, Eden? You'll be going home soon. You'll be the Eden we once knew, just that much more."

"Home. I'm longing to go back home," Nicholas uttered. "This life has been too inferior."

A crash came through the door. Quinn charged through the rubble as the wind picked up speed again and blew the outside life inside.

"You made it," I said to him, catching my breath. My head still throbbed, although not as hard.

"*What happened to you?* Are you all right?" He helped me to my feet. Quinn grabbed a chair and settled me into it.

"I'm sorry about everything. I shouldn't have come," I said to him. "I was wrong."

"Quinn, I was wondering when I'd see you again. It's been a lifetime," Horus said.

"Horus? Why are you here?" Quinn looked at Mom, then at Nicholas and Mercedes.

"Helen and I had an arrangement, but there were alterations that needed to be addressed. The big picture, as you would say, was overlooked." He turned to Mom with wisdom masked across his face. "In due time, your powers may be stripped. I leave that up to Raefield. For now, I have what I need."

"Horus . . . *no*. You're making a big mistake. Raefield will not grant you your freedom. He needs you too much. He'll never let you go. I know you believe that. You have to," Mom pleaded.

"There's nothing I can do. It's already set in motion."

"You're not taking—"

The West Virginia witches stood firm and quickly moved toward Quinn when he grabbed my arm and tried to force his way through. They surrounded him and secured the scene.

"Get him. *Grrr*. Take his arm before he gets away."

"Strike him if n-n-necessary if he tries anything. He thinks we can't fight."

"Grab her mother, too. Sh-she's clever."

They charged us. I recognized a ring on the hand of one of the assailants. Several foolish witches wore the same ring. They were only pawns in a bigger plan.

"*Quinn*, I'm sorry. You can't fight it. Nobody can." I pleaded with them to loosen their grip on him. I attempted to stay focused to keep any hope alive. "Please, you already have me. Let them safely go."

"This journey is not for them. That will be decided at a later time. It's nearing," Horus said with a stony face.

"Lauren, don't. You can fight it," Quinn pleaded and tried to free himself of their grip. He began wielding his strength.

Another energy charge took over. The room rattled like the

quakes we'd experienced earlier on the streets of Chicago. This time, I knew the reason. The time of change neared. My headaches before the quakes and Mom's sense of something not right had predicted this event. Even Chelsea experienced warnings. The outside energy connected with me. I felt its strength, strong and exhilarating. The energy took hold of me, and I took hold of the lasting energy.

"Huh!" My body floated in the air.

"Lauren!" Quinn yelled. He ran to me, but couldn't penetrate the unbreakable barrier.

I fell to the ground. I gasped for air. My head throbbed. The energy force raged mercilessly inside. The gem lit up, now fully awake and alive. When the pain subsided, I lifted myself off the floor.

Mom managed to free herself from the witches. She moved towards me, but a force stopped her from reaching me. She pounded on the wall that connected me to my newfound bond. We were locked together in an invisible vault.

"I'm sorry. I can't control it. It's connected to me."

"Lauren, break free!" Quinn called out.

Every item in the bookstore not weighted down blew everywhere. Change would happen. I couldn't escape.

"It's too great. Like the message said. It's the storm," I said to him.

"What are you talking about?" Quinn shouted through the quagmire.

"The Coming Storm. I'm the coming storm. I'm the one that brought this change. I'm the one that's opening the portal."

I saw the grin and satisfaction on Horus's face. The student had finally solved the equation. The student now became the teacher. Everything fell into mathematical sequence.

"That's right. You are calling it open. You're at the right time, at the right place when the harvest is great. Nature is responding to your calls. The door is opening," Horus replied.

I heard my mother crying, a paradigm of two women coming together. "You knew I would come even after Mom offered the sacrifice. You never planned to take it, because I would come. How did you know this would happen?"

"It was written. Raefield knew that a great mist was expected on this very day and it would somehow bind with a special entity, causing a collision of forces. That force is you. The rest was pure chance and speculation. Her parents knew as well," Horus explained to us righteously.

"Lauren, I won't lose you again!" Quinn shouted. His cries became muted by the energy and the heaviness that engulfed the room.

The fabric that held me in bondage suddenly burst to form the great blue mist of the stories I had heard and the nightmares I knew would come. Everyone in the room fell over from the power of the mist.

"Nooo!" Quinn shouted through the chaos.

My body toppled backwards by the sheer force of the mist. A hand grabbed me as I fell. Horus managed to maneuver inside the secured vault when a weakness opened up during the transformation into the mist.

Mercedes laughed. She had grabbed onto Horus and pulled Nicholas along when the mist opened. We were now protected inside. The West Virginia clan surrounded the remaining people left outside. Leslie helped Aaron up. I knew Mom, Quinn and the Brandts could fight them.

"What about us?" asked a witch. He looked enviously at two witches who'd managed to pass through the mist.

"Sorry, maybe next time," Mercedes told them. "We appreciate your help."

I reached out to the ones in my heart. *"Mom . . . Quinn."*

Mom struggled, her face covered with tears. *"Break free, Lauren. We'll find you!"*

"Lauren!" Quinn called out, his voice dimmed. He tried to break into the mist one more time.

"I love you. Always," I said, my voice cracked. I raised my hand to meet his across the mist, never making contact.

In an instant, the mist moved. We were pulled into the air away from everyone I had known until the people in the store turned into flashes of light and imaginary particles that trickled through my fingertips.

15

REVERSION

I don't know if my head spun too fast or this machine wouldn't stop spinning, and maybe from shutting my eyes, the light-headed increased, which caused me to become disoriented and fall. A boney hand firmly grasped mine. I looked up to see a figure losing form. The skin on the man peeled and melted away and his hair turned thin and ghastly white, which blew in the wind. His organs remained intact. He smiled at me through his skeletal face and bulging white eyes.

"Huh!" I still gripped his boney hand, afraid to let go and slip into another break in time, lost forever. I thought about Quinn and my mother.

"You won't fall, my dear, but it's just as well that I hold onto you," Horus said to me with those crazy eyes.

I quickly looked away, ashamed and scared to stare at a man I'd once thought handsome, a man who killed an innocent to gain my attention. I turned back and studied the two main bones of his arm, up to the tubular one that somehow supported me. I pulled away, but the skeleton kept his firm grip on me. He held me tight, just as strong as the body it shed. Horus smiled fervently again.

My feet floated freely, so I knew the safety of the mist still held us in place. We wouldn't fall. I understood the mist's purpose and protection. Regarding freedom? I became a prisoner.

I looked up at Mercedes and Nicholas. She took on the role as queen of the ship, ready to come into her realm at the end of this voyage. Nicholas looked indifferent as always. He was the unfazed seasoned traveler. He looked at me and grinned, a wicked and rightful smile. My stomach dropped.

"Isn't this wonderful? You're going home. I'm going home. I'm going to be free," Horus said to me.

I kept my mouth shut. I refused to say anything to the murderer or the rest of this harrowing crew. How could I? I was being kidnapped!

"Don't look so distraught, my dear. It's a wonderful place. You'll see that Raefield can be very accommodating," Mercedes chimed in. Her dark mane blew in the wind. She really did believe she was the maiden queen.

I stared at the two scavenger witches, all giddy and excited about their prospect of a new life. Little did they know they'd only become pawns and servants to His Majesty. I checked the walls of the mist. It appeared translucent and flimsy. How could it possibly hold us? I knew what I needed to do. I closed my eyes and forced my mind to bring forth the dormant life inside of me.

The energy released.

"It won't work in here. The mist trumps us all," the skeletal voice said to me.

I opened my eyes but refused to let him see my frustration. I refocused again and called to the source. The energy moved once more, harder and stronger. I felt the surge rip through me in an electrifying manner. I had awakened the power, and it waited for my next summons.

"You're wasting valuable energy. It will just go to the surface and dissipate. You'll weaken yourself," Horus said. "Balance is everything within the mist."

I ignored him again and pushed even further. This time, the energy released at full capacity and pushed right out of me. It felt intoxicating. The energy sat out in the periphery and waited for my command. Then, it stalled. I couldn't direct the energy. I lost the ability to guide the force. The energy had no place to go, so it ricocheted back into me. I fell over.

Horus let go of my hand. "Please do try to listen to me. It's for your own good."

I couldn't let him see the defeat in my eyes, nor the anger and humiliation brewing. How stupid of me to fall right into what they had planned all along. The warnings had surrounded me all this time, and I'd chosen to exercise my free will, thinking I could help everyone. Now everything felt lost.

Mercedes looked over at me with righteousness. "It'll be a new beginning. You can let go of your old life and everyone who thought they were doing you a favor. This will pass, and you'll barely remember any of them."

"How can I forget them? They were real, and they were my family and friends. Something you've never had and never will!"

Mercedes looked away.

"Do you think in Raefield's world it'll be better? Once he conquers everyone outside of his circle, he'll keep his stranglehold on all of you. Just like he does now. None of you will ever be free, only at his mercy. You know that."

Horus turned to me as if I spoke some obscure language. "You don't know him, but you will."

"You don't know what you're talking about. We're not servants of Raefield, but his allies," Mercedes scoffed at me. *"Can't you put a muzzle on her?"*

The skeleton of Horus looked seriously amused. He turned away and faced forward as the journey continued. I knew we neared my nightmare. The pain traveled throughout my body, but all I could think about was my family and friends left behind.

And of my broken heart.

Quinn.

*

I opened my eyes to the bad dream that now consumed my life. I knew exactly where we landed. The electrical energy shifted inside of me again, but something else felt different. My hair grew longer and my clothes felt tighter. The curves on my hips seemed more noticeable. I looked up at Horus, who now merged in full form. He appeared younger than after we had left New Haven. Even Mercedes and Nicholas looked more youthful. The indentations on Nicholas' face faded.

"Are we here? Are we here?" exclaimed one of the witches. They didn't seem to change much in age or appearance. "Mercedes, you look . . . different."

"Well, of course, I do, you mindless fool! I knew I would come out radiant." She pushed her way to the front. "I need a mirror."

Horus turned to me and grinned with his mouth intact. His body was now completely covered in regenerated skin and a fine robe to match. He resonated confidence and masculinity. I felt uneasy, knowing the man who would turn me over to Raefield commanded a lure.

"Lauren, what a sight you are. Definitely more mature, but lovely as always. I would say youth remains even with the added years," he remarked with a coquettish laugh. "But we're in Raefield's land, and we can't have you using any persuasive ideas."

Before I could take any steps forward, four guards appeared out of nowhere and rushed to my side. They bound my hands behind my back with weighted chains that I couldn't break.

"His land. They're much stronger."

"Grrr." I shifted from side to side against the grips of the obedient guards. The chains tightened every time I tried to break free. "Is this how you treat a guest?"

"When we know you can be trusted, then you'll get a little more freedom. In the meantime, until your energy drains, I think it's wise not to give you too much latitude. You're his guest now. You'll behave accordingly."

"Or, do you mean if I don't do what you want, you might not get your freedom from Raefield."

Horus gave me sharp look. His lips then curved upward. "My salvation awaits me."

"He won't keep his word."

He stopped again and pursed his lips. "Some advice you should strongly consider. Don't make this harder for yourself. It's best you do as he wishes."

"And what if I don't?"

"I don't wish any harm to you. This is your life now, Lauren. You belong here. Let go of that past."

How could he ask that of me when I'd just been robbed of everything that was important and taken somewhere far away that no one could reach? I tried not to slip into the reaches of insanity as I wrapped my mind around the idea of living in another time and never seeing the people I cared about.

"In time, you will fall into place."

I trailed a few steps behind Horus toward my new forsaken life. My heart sank deeper into my chest. I would close it off. It was the only way. Raefield awaited me at the end of this jaded rainbow of doom.

"When do we get to see him?" asked one of the lost witches.

Horus stopped instantly. He quickly spun around to the end of this malignant formation. "Very soon, my little imps. You'll witness his greatness. Take caution not to bother him or find your throats at the end of his reach." The two outcast witches flinched. Horus gazed over at me before moving ahead to the grim outlook in front of us.

Raefield's people met us at the door. "My dear Eden, you've returned to us in full form. How wickedly lovely you've turned out," a woman cooed. "You've been away for *tooo* long."

"It's Lauren now. And I don't plan on staying."

The dark-haired witch giggled. "Yes, we've been briefed on your feistiness. And the name preference . . . it'll take some time to be accustomed to. Once you settle in, it'll feel like you've never left. Eden will rise."

I hid my irritation. *Must. Preserve. Energy.*

"Ah, Eden . . . I mean Lauren. Welcome back. You must be tired from your long journey. We've been waiting for you." The man motioned to the four guards, and in seconds, they disappeared as fast as they had appeared. "That's better. Excuse us for the formality. One can't be too certain of any hasty reaction once coming through the mist."

"You mean me? No, I think you've covered it with the chains."

The formal man laughed. "You must understand the prowess of your own strength. Raefield would not like a . . . commotion."

"Of course."

"Please, come this way. There are people killing to meet you."

Quinn, please find me . . . fast.

I walked into the grand estate, through its foreboding doors, and into the nest of my most despised nemesis. My chaperones gladly escorted me into his domain as their victorious prize. The hunters had ceased and captured, the hunted finally caught.

"You'll enjoy his home. All wicked are welcome!" the dark-haired beauty laughed.

The man cleared his throat. "You'll have to excuse Imani. She gets excited when a new arrival comes to his greatness. It's not everyday you come home. She can teach you a great deal."

"I see. Would that be useful in my escape?"

The man chuckled. "Please, you must let that notion go. I'm sure it may feel difficult for you to be here, but once everything becomes clearer, the desire to escape will leave you." The man looked sympathetic. "I am Jaxson. We'll be with you in transition."

I swallowed hard. We moved through the high-ceilinged foyer and around the paired, granite staircase. A very large room approached. I remembered it during my thoughtless trip into his den that night in New Haven. I swear I heard voices rising. . . .

Bright light flashed into my eyes and disappeared. I looked down at my arms and body. I was suddenly draped in an eloquent cream-colored dress that fit perfectly against my hips and torso. My hair was pulled back, and I wore strapped shoes that made me taller.

"This way," Jaxson said as we neared the great room.

The room looked bright and airy and grand in its décor, yet suitable for guests to enjoy unlike a museum of untouchables. Every head turned to face me with widened eyes and mouths gaping. Fifteen chatty strangers suddenly fell silent. I flushed. Fear gripped me. The back of a man kissing Mercedes passionately caught my attention. The knot in my stomach tightened.

Mercedes finally opened her eyes to catch her breath after the man gently released her. Her deep eyes penetrated me. "Lauren! We've been waiting." She motioned for me to come forward.

The man turned around. His bright eyes glistened as he gazed at me. A radiant smile matched his glowing face, and his glossed, light hair shimmered in the sunlight. His rosy cheeks depicted a joyful man.

All I saw was the devil.

"Eden," Raefield whispered.

ACKNOWLEDGMENTS

Balancing writing and life is never easy, especially when trying to put together another piece of work into something I can be proud of and readers can enjoy. Assistance is always needed and appreciated in editing, publishing, marketing and promoting, designing, or just moral support to push me through. I'm grateful to many supporters and readers, but I'd like to acknowledge people that have really pulled through for me, including new ones to the list.

A big thank you: Laura Taylor, James T. Egan and Kira Rubenthaler of Bookfly Design, Diana Padgett, Becky May and Lola May's, Elizabeth Duong, Tien Vo, Cindy Matalucci and Elite Networking, Peter Tran, Jade Suong Nguyen and Nails!America, Jennifer Ebner, Traci Wilkerson Steckel, Indy Quillen, Evan Ramspott, Cammie Noelle and La Marque Café, Crystal Carr, Bri Geeski, Stacey Dyson, Austin Farmer, Jennifer Beckman, Lucinda Campbell, and my family.

Shout out to: Veronica Bueno, Donna Dreyer, Margarette Borg, and Odette Crandall — You ladies crack me up.

Always grateful: Carolyn Burch and Angela Johnson — Long running friends are like gold.

Sharp Grossmont Hospital, especially 3East — You guys rock!

CPSIA information can be obtained
at www.ICGtesting.com
Printed in the USA
LVHW110256061118
596089LV00001B/115/P